UNEXPECTED CHILD

Also by Patricia Grossman

<u>For Adults</u>

Four Figures in Time
Inventions in a Grieving House

<u>For Children</u>

Saturday Market
The Night Ones

UNEXPECTED CHILD

PATRICIA GROSSMAN

alyson books
los angeles | new york

MANUFACTURED IN THE UNITED STATES OF AMERICA.

THIS TRADE PAPERBACK ORIGINAL IS PUBLISHED BY ALYSON PUBLICATIONS,
P.O. BOX 4371, LOS ANGELES, CA 90078-4371.
DISTRIBUTION IN THE UNITED KINGDOM BY
TURNAROUND PUBLISHER SERVICES LTD.,
UNIT 3, OLYMPIA TRADING ESTATE, COBURG ROAD, WOOD GREEN,
LONDON N22 6TZ ENGLAND.

FIRST EDITION: DECEMBER 2000

00 01 02 03 04 **a** 10 9 8 7 6 5 4 3 2 1

ISBN: 1-55583-544-9

LIBRARY OF CONGRESS CATALOGING-IN-PUBLICATION DATA
GROSSMAN, PATRICIA.
UNEXPECTED CHILD / PATRICIA GROSSMAN.—1ST ED.
ISBN 1-55583-544-9
1. LESBIAN MOTHERS—FICTION. 2. ADOPTED CHILDREN—FICTION. I. TITLE
PS3557.R6726 U54 2000
813'.54—DC21   00-045400

COVER PHOTOGRAPHY AND DESIGN BY PHILIP PIROLO.

As always, for Helene, and for Jeffrey Aronoff

1

"My name is Meg Krantz. I'm a volunteer at REACH. I know it's taken forever to get back to you, and I'm sorry. But I'm going to be working with you and Kimble, and I'd love for us to set up an appointment."

"Oh, yeah. REACH. Jesus. So you finally reached over here."

"I do apologize, Mr. Toffler. I know it's probably been frustrating for you."

"Yeah, well, hey, look—"

"Can we set something up?"

"Sure. You people aren't so bad. I've heard worse, believe me."

"Now, how are you feeling these days? Would you like to meet, or shall I come to you?"

"I was in St. Luke's, ya know. Respiratory stuff. I'm out now."

"Uh-huh," said Meg. "What sort of respiratory trouble?"

"Nah, not TB, don't worry. My culture was good. Anyway, hey, I'd do the quarantine. First they thought it was bacterial, then they thought it was PCP, then they thought it was viral.

The fancier their machines get, the dumber they get."

"So would you like me to come to you?"

"We can meet. I'm going stir-crazy sittin' here all day, ya know?" Barry held the receiver away. "Kimmy, we're gonna go out and meet a nice lady, OK?" Meg heard a clicking sound, like a Zippo lighter being snapped on and off. "She's watching her Mr. Rogers. Mr. Goody Two-Shoes. If anyone used that mealy-mouthed voice on me when I was a kid, I woulda made sure he got real."

Meg had not intended to meet Barry and his daughter Kimble that day, but she found herself reluctant to correct his impression. "Here's an idea," she said. "Is it any trouble for you to get to the Central Park Zoo?"

"No, couple of transfers is all. What else is new? Gimme a time an' place."

"Say, by Seal Island at 2 o'clock? Is that enough time for you?"

"We can do it. You gonna be wearing a REACH T-shirt or what?"

Meg disliked T-shirts with writing on them. It had always struck her as sad that people chose to identify themselves in the minds of strangers by the slogans or endorsements on their T-shirts. The last gay pride march she attended was full of women wearing T-shirts with boldly printed assertions: LOVE MAKES A FAMILY or WE'RE NOT JUST FRIENDS. Meg had always blanched at such overweening declarations.

"No, but I have very curly hair, practically red, about shoulder length. I'll wear a blue sweater."

"You'll know me, no problem. The cane's a dead giveaway. Hey, thanks for callin'. I know you guys there do your job. Listen, I'm quick to accuse, quick to forgive. Just call me 'Quick.' Except not these days."

Meg laughed. "Well, I'm looking forward to meeting you and Kimble. Kimmy?"

"Whatever. Her mother called her Kimble. That's her real name. Her mother wanted something different, who the hell knows why. I said Katherine or Kimberly were perfectly fine, but what do I know, right?"

For the first time since Meg began volunteering six years ago in 1983, she had called her client without first going into the REACH office to read the intake report. Too many times in the past she had found the intake reports, drawn up by lay clinicians, to be weighted with editorial declarations that had no bearing on the client's case. Sometimes the reports even contained gross errors. Meg suspected that the clinicians, fearful of being found out in their sloppy note-taking, cheated on what they regarded as mere details. Once she had read in a new client's report that his lover Benjamin had recently died. When Meg had later offered condolences, she discovered that Benjamin was a distant friend who had died three years before, while the client's healthy lover of 12 years had just walked out on him. Fortunately, the client himself had saved the day. "Thanks, doll," he had exclaimed. "It's refreshing to think of maggots running across Carston's eyes as we speak."

The Tofflers, Barry and Kimble, were the first related clients Meg would have. She had wanted a change, and Tina at REACH was happy to accommodate. Doubtlessly confident that Meg would scrutinize the eight-page intake report before she called the client, Tina had provided only the bare-bones information laid out on the referral sheet. Meg found out that Barry was an ex-IV user with a prison record and had been in recovery for nine years. His wife Anita had died two years before. His daughter was four-and-a-half years old and

HIV-negative. He needed help with household chores. He need-
ed to get his daughter "fixed up." "Fixed up" is all he would say,
Tina claimed. "Financial?" Meg had inquired. "No problem,"
Tina had responded. "He was a mason. Good union benefits."

∞   ∞   ∞

In front of Seal Island, Meg smiled broadly and waved her
arm in the direction of a man walking with a cane and the little
girl skipping in front of him. With his free hand, Barry saluted
Meg. Then he called to the child, who ran once around him
and stopped. He licked his thumb and wiped something off her
cheek. This overtly maternal gesture was more than Meg could
bear. Guiltily, she wondered if it was orchestrated for effect.
The language of manipulation designed by addicts, former and
present, was a romance language: It seduced with florid expressions and bathetic gestures.

Barry reached Meg. Because he was shorter than she had
imagined and the child taller, an air of alliance had been established between father and daughter. Kimble plied herself
against Barry's leg, stuck her thumb in her mouth, and stared
up at Meg. At first sight her looks were neither pretty nor
homely. She was ethereal. Her blond hair had retained its baby
texture; it was flaxen and flyaway like the hair of cherubs in
Romantic paintings. The skin of her temples was translucent.
Meg noticed one winding, pale-blue vein, unwitting testament
to the fragility of her circumstances. The lips that protruded
around her thumb were defiantly rosy. Her Victorian dress, imitation Laura Ashley, was clearly chosen by an unstylish man trying to draw out of his daughter the reputed femininity of little
girls. When Meg looked down at Kimble, she felt her face
flame; she was nearly afraid. She could not remember the last

time she had confronted a child's frank stare. Had she ever been so unnerved as this afternoon by the dead certainty that children know all that has to be known? Meg was deciding how to greet Kimble when the little girl removed her thumb from her mouth and said, "Seals."

"Jesus, Kimmy. Say hello to the nice lady. Say 'My name is Kimble Toffler. It's nice to meet you.'"

Kimble put her thumb back in her mouth.

Meg laughed. "It's nice to meet you." She extended her hand to Barry. "I'm Meg Krantz."

Barry shook Meg's hand. "Likewise." He looked at his own frail arm. "I used to have muscle mass. You wouldn't believe it now."

Meg nodded. Barry was about 5 feet 9 inches. He appeared to weigh little over 100. His hair, like Kimble's, seemed thin in an untimely way. Yet Barry had a firm, square jaw—a Dick Tracy jaw, a jaw that inspired confidence. Muscle mass was easy to imagine.

"*Seals,*" demanded Kimble.

"OK, honey," said Barry. "Seals."

Together, Meg and Barry turned around and leaned on the railing to watch the seals travel their monotonous course.

"Up," demanded Kimble.

All color drained from Barry's face. He fumbled with his cane and did not look at Meg.

Meg got behind Kimble, put her hands under her arms, and hoisted her to a position where she could wait for a seal to emerge from under the water and pirouette in front of them. Sidling up close, she braced the little girl with her arms to prevent her from falling backward. It was a presumptuous pose to take with a strange child, a child who knew all there was to know, a child of whom Meg was nearly afraid.

All three stood like that together, with Meg acting as buttress for Kimble and Barry watching on his own. After a while an old, whiskered seal pushed its head above the water and yowled. It did this several times, each time it passed. Without glancing at Meg or at his daughter, Barry watched for the old seal to come around, to surface once again. Then he arched his back and pitched a desperate plea timed to harmonize with the seal's. It achieved its mark perfectly. Kimble laughed and laughed—one joyous shout colliding into another. Meg was surrounded by noise: the seal's bark, Barry's echo, Kimble's laughter. She was surprised at how easily grief and delight mingled their sounds.

∞   ∞   ∞

At an uptown restaurant with her mother, Meg put a hard roll on her bread plate, unwrapped the foil wrapper over a single pad of sweet butter, and announced in an even tone that Jerry had died three weeks before, had essentially drowned in the fluid produced by his own lungs.

"It's certainly a shame," said Charlotte. "But I don't honestly know what to say. This was inevitable from the start. Am I right?"

Immediately Meg called up Libby's advice: "Don't let the old dame get away with it."

Meg had been seeing Libby twice a week for the past nine months. Libby was herself an "old dame," although Meg did not know how old. She had received her training, the specifics of which Meg could not quite recall, during the second half of her life. On a single-minded quest to get Meg to tell her mother off, Libby tempted her by describing the elevated states of mind she would achieve once the deed was done. Meg had made it a

mission to negotiate a compromise between Libby's advice and
her own sense of what could be borne. In session after session
Meg had articulated in precise terms why she could not go
beyond a certain point with Charlotte, a widow whose only
child was Meg. "What are you protecting her for?" Libby had
snapped. "She can take it. Her life is just dandy. She's a fortunate woman. It's *your* life that's wanting." The answer that had
sprung to Meg's mind—"She's *old*"—was the one prohibited
answer.

At the restaurant Charlotte busied herself with buttering
her roll, then pushing small objects—bud vase, cut-glass salt
shaker—about the table. Meg watched.

"I'm sorry if I sound harsh, Meg, but you took on Jerry as a
dying man, and now he's died. It's not that it isn't sad."

Their Caesar salads had come. *It's only once a month,* Meg
thought. *These fucking lunches,* she thought, making sure to
savor the silent pronunciation of "fucking," *are only once a
month.* Yet she could already hear Libby during their next session, "Whadidya *tell* her for? It's none of her business about
Jerry. Your life is none of her business." Then she would calm
down, assume the role of a real therapist. "I wonder what you
wanted from her," she would say, her heart clearly not in it. "I
wonder what you wanted to get from her in that moment."

For years Charlotte had not understood Meg's commitment
to REACH, to putting herself out for dying strangers. Several
times she had suggested that Meg might be trying to fill a void.
("Just drop her a little hint *what* void you're trying to fill," Libby
had advised. "She'll run for the hills, I guarantee it.")

"Jerry was a wonderful man," Meg said. "An amazing man,
actually." Despite her effort to prevent it, her voice shook.

Charlotte adjusted herself in her seat. She sat half up,
smoothed out the back of her skirt, a Chanel, and sat down again.

Meg looked at the skirt that fell evenly over her mother's lap. So much of it came down to clothes with Meg and Charlotte. When Meg was growing up in New York, in the same Park Avenue apartment where Charlotte lived now, her mother's life was dominated by clothes. When as a child Meg thought about her mother, she thought of clothes and of accessories. More specifically, she thought of department stores, those vast and twinkling shrines to capitalism that beckoned her mother over and again. Charlotte entered the Fifth Avenue stores with as much purposeful zeal when she was returning a garment as when she was purchasing one. Indeed, for years Meg had thought the purpose of making a purchase was to return it. She had told Libby it would have been one thing if Charlotte indulged only herself, but she was forever buying and returning outfits for Meg. Although her standards for these purchases never varied (she did not consider blends and stayed strictly away from the mauves and pastels that "backed Meg into the wallpaper"), she always found a reason to make an exchange: patterns that turned out to be printed and not woven through, buttonholes not well-reinforced, darts a shade too obvious, yokes of dubious craftsmanship. Meg despised the clothes her mother selected, but her protests were so energetically squelched that she soon enough lost the will to assert herself. Rather, Meg began to meet up with a disproportionate number of accidents. Iodine covering a cut bled through new linen shorts. A goat from a petting zoo nibbled at the bib of a new woolen jumper. Later, when Meg was older, the billowing skirt of a dress bought for a prom she did not want to attend got caught in the whirling blades of a fan. Libby had reproached Meg for these accidents. These accidents, she claimed, had set the stage for her current inability to simply and crisply speak the truth.

"Jerry must have been a wonderful man," Charlotte now said. "Otherwise, you wouldn't have thought so."

Meg laid down her fork. She was through eating.

Charlotte, who ate slower, looked up. "I don't mean to trivialize your relationship with him. Or what you've been through. I'm sorry if I did that."

The word *trivialize* was particularly galling—a deliberate sideswipe into Meg's generation.

"Now that it's over, maybe you can take a break for a while," Charlotte said. "Develop the business a little more. What about stepping up your mail order, like you planned? Everyone who comes into my apartment adores your pots."

"Business is good. Orders are up 15% this year. I'm doing fine."

"Well, then it's a particularly good time to branch out. Success begets success. Unless, of course, you don't want to. Maybe you're not interested in that kind of scale."

"I'm not, actually."

"Ambition is not the most important thing, is it? That's the area in which your father was so excessive. Ambition. I suppose it was a typical failing for the times. Men then didn't understand ambition isn't everything."

"Excuse me. They do now?"

Charlotte removed her napkin to the table and smoothed it out. "Please, Meg." She turned her attention to Madison Avenue.

Their table was placed just inside French doors that opened onto the sidewalk. Charlotte always chose to be seated right in the midst of some pedestrian artery. During their winter lunches, she liked to be placed along the main aisle so she could see the maître d' usher couples and small groups to their seats. No matter how closely passersby might represent the typical looks of her own milieu, Charlotte would sight each one with the glee of a child spotting a friendly animal along the road. The members of her species intrigued her, and her enthusiasm for them contributed to her youthful appearance. She was 73 and highly impressionable.

"So when are you leaving?"

Charlotte was going on a cruise to the Galapagos. She was going with Ida Tree, a neighbor in her apartment building, and Ida's daughter, Juliet, who had just gotten a divorce. In repeated phone conversations Charlotte had stressed how rejuvenating the trip would be for Juliet, who had lost her White Plains house because of her husband's slick lawyer.

Charlotte opened her purse and removed a trip itinerary and a brochure showcasing the cruise. She pointed out some pictures of birds and animals with startling appearances. One seabird had bright-blue webbed feet.

"Wow," said Meg. "This is going to be really great."

"Are you sure we can't entice you? It's not too late, you know."

"No. No, thank you. This is my big fair season, remember? Sullivan County, Rhinebeck, Somerset. It's my busiest time."

"We won't be going for a month. Juliet would be thrilled if you came."

"Somerset is in a month. I really can't."

Meg knew Juliet. Ida Tree's daughter had found a way to live in politely cultivated angst. To her, female friends were ones who would cooperate in an endless disclosure of marital humiliations. Juliet's ideal confidante would be a woman whose husband's slick lawyer had just robbed her of her White Plains house.

"Can't you skip Somerset one year? This is a once-in-a-life-time opportunity. You know I'd help you out. I just got a surprise premium." Here, Charlotte did not speak; she trilled.

"Mom, you were just talking about my developing the business. I can't take off that kind of time."

With some effort Meg probably could make the arrangements to go along. Yet, although the Galapagos held for her a rich and exotic appeal, she could think of nothing more prosaic than listening to Charlotte, Ida, and Juliet discussing past and fleeing husbands. It was easy enough for Meg to envision the scene: She would remain silent, politely electing not to allude to the condition of her invisibility in their presence.

"I suppose not," conceded Charlotte. Her voice abruptly lost its timbre.

Without fail, this attenuated version of Charlotte's voice snaked its way into Meg's blood. ("Why do I feel it so strongly?" Meg had demanded of Libby. "How can even the suggestion of her sadness cripple me?" Meg had expected Libby to point out that Charlotte's manipulations never missed their mark, that she was a guileful old broad who left bodies by the roadside. Rather, she had leaned forward in her leather swivel chair, steadied herself with the toe of her high-heel shoe, and confided, "Because you feel so sorry for yourself.")

"It's not just the fairs," Meg claimed now. "I've already started with another client. A man with a daughter. It should be a very different kind of experience. I guess it's my way of dealing with Jerry. I know. I'm a little crazed."

Charlotte's eyes were hidden behind the laminated card of the dessert menu. Meg expected her to remark on the term *client*. She had once commented that in the past only lawyers had clients. Now manicurists and party clowns and everyone on God's earth had them. But Charlotte was distracted. "I'm having the key lime pie," she said, "and you're having the white chocolate mousse so I can have a taste."

"Fine," agreed Meg. She smiled. When the mousse arrived,

white and brown chocolate shavings touting its extravagance, Meg offered her mother the first taste. She leaned over to poise the spoon within reach of Charlotte's mouth, a gesture so long abandoned that both their faces blazed. At once they began a frenzied discussion of mousses they had tasted over the years. They were in perfect accord; they extolled and dismissed the very same mousses until the waiter came and placed between them a silver tray bearing the check and two Godiva chocolates.

2

"I barter in fertility goddesses," Meg told people when they asked what she did. It was close to the truth. For eight years she had been selling her pottery at trade and crafts shows around the tristate area. In the last two years the fertility goddesses had attracted some attention and provided a steady income. Flower pitchers with Artemis handles, bowls decorated with images of Hera in childbirth, vessel lids in the shape of Juno, jugs with Demeter spouts—all had taken off in the last two years.

Rather than celebrate the success to which she had long aspired, Meg worried that the profitability of the pots detracted from their artistic value. She worried that she might be exploiting their buyers. Invariably, the great majority of people who bought her fertility pots were women who were trying to get pregnant. Meg made no claim for the power of the pots, but these women bought. In the suburbs they bought in droves.

Today, two weeks after she had met Barry and Kimble at the Central Park Zoo, Meg prepared for a crafts festival in Sullivan County. Her van, illegally parked in front of her building on Duane Street, was filled to the roof with boxes of fertility goddesses swathed in bubble wrap. Just as Meg emerged from the freight elevator to get the final load, she heard the voice of Tina from REACH on the answering machine. She picked up. "I'm here. What's going on?"

"We have a bit of a problem. Your client has gone into St. Luke's again, and his little girl doesn't have anyone to take care of her."

"Shit. What's wrong with him?"

"They don't know, but he has a fever of 104. The social worker from St. Luke's called. Apparently he didn't bring your number with him. The little girl was going to stay with her grandmother, but something went wrong."

Meg knew all about Grandma Shirl. Barry had spoken about her at length that day at the zoo. They had sat together on a bench, eating soft cones while Kimble chased pigeons. He had said that if he were in any kind of shape, he wouldn't take that woman's crap for ten seconds. Bam, he said, he'd be outta there. Grandma Shirl detested Barry, but she was Kimble's only connection to her mother. She cared for Kimble when Barry could not. Barry said she was good to Kimble. Sleeping atop the huge fluffy feather bed in front of the TV in the Rego Park apartment, Kimble looked like an angel. Grandma Shirl made her whatever she asked for: peanut butter and bananas on toast, tuna melts, cupcakes with Gummi Bears trapped neck-high in peaks of frosting. She painted Kimble's toenails with glitter polish, each toe a different color. When Barry appeared to claim his daughter, his mother-in-law threatened to have a restraining order put on him, though she could not come up with a just cause. But even as she wanted to keep Barry from Kimble, she complained she was too weary to start all over with a little girl.

As Barry had spoken, his shoulders had hunched forward. Meg had sensed the last vestige of the day's energy stream out of him. "Who can blame her? She ought to just shoot me...put me outta my misery. Do the world a favor."

Meg had argued with Barry, told him he could not let Grandma Shirl get away with hating him instead of hating the disease; he must not for a moment take her scorn to heart; he could not turn his limited energy against himself; he had too much to do, too much to look after. Then she had watched her words take hold. Barry's eyes misted in acknowledgment of her impulsive allegiance. His gaze held onto hers. As before with very sick clients, Meg saw that Barry viewed her good health as evidence that she had succeeded where he had failed, that she had the power to create the magical balance of energies required to produce wholeness. His gaze expected more. Meg had no more to give. She had fallen silent, leaving the suggestion of her uncertainty in the air between them. In truth, she had suddenly imagined herself as Grandma Shirl, a middle-class elderly woman whose only daughter had died a few months after an ex-junkie had infected her.

Now on the phone with Tina at REACH, Meg felt stymied. "Jesus," she said. "You don't know what went wrong with the grandmother?"

"No. The little girl's at a neighbor's, but she can't stay there."

"All right. I have to go upstate, but I'll take her with me."

"For how long?" Tina asked. "We really can't have you doing this."

"Uh-huh. And why did you call me, then? What am I supposed to do?"

Tina lowered her voice. "We need to think about placement for the little girl. Her situation is just too tentative. We're extremely grateful to you, Meg, but this absolutely cannot happen again. While you're upstate I'm going to keep trying to find the grandmother. You keep trying too. Call me as soon as you know something. We have to get right on some permanency planning."

Over the last year Meg's minivan had proven too small for her inventory; she had gotten into the habit of stacking several boxes of goddesses into the passenger seat, securing them with the shoulder harness and several lengths of rope. Today she left the last goddesses behind and drove uptown, her passenger seat empty. Along the way, it occurred to her that Kimble might not have a suitable country outfit or anything besides Victorian print dresses with billowing skirts. At Union Square Meg parked the van in a garage and went into May's. There she bought Kimble a Little Mermaid overnight bag with a pocket mirror and a toothbrush hanging from a vinyl loop. She bought a pair of overalls, two T-shirts, a package of underwear in what seemed a reasonable size, and rubber sandals. As an after-thought she ran back and selected a clear plastic rain slicker. These she folded into the overnight bag and got back into the van. Resuming her journey, Meg felt a vague buzz of regret. Who was she to remake wispy little Kimble into some barely considered image of a four-year-old?

A half hour later Meg introduced herself to Barry's neigh-bor, who called herself Honey. Honey had four children under the age of seven and seemed utterly relieved to see Meg. She told her REACH had been good to her brother three years before. Without being summoned, Kimble emerged from a noisy room deep within the apartment. She was flushed and wore the same Victorian dress Barry had dressed her in the day Meg had met them at the zoo. She pointed to Meg. "Seals."

"Hi, Kimble. Do you like to be called Kimble or Kimmy?"

Kimble shrugged.

"Have you ever been to the country? I'm taking you to the

country. No seals, but deer. Have you ever seen a deer? Bambi?"

"Daddy's sick. Grandma Shirl's gambling. She's a *gambler*." Kimble sucked in an admiring breath.

Honey clicked her tongue. "That's right enough. She takes one of those double-decker buses to Atlantic City or Cherokee, North Carolina, or who knows where else. Every chance she gets." Honey gave Meg a quick once-over, apparently judged her worthy, and said, "Some people got their priorities up the A-S-S-H-O-L-E."

"A-S-S…" began Kimble.

"…spells you're outta here," said Honey. "This nice lady's gonna take you to the country, and you're one lucky little girl."

Halfway up the Palisades, Kimble stared ahead, not visibly blinking. Meg was alarmed. It came upon her that Kimble had never seen either of her parents healthy. Did she accept it as a given that the people in her orbit were less able than others? How did she imagine Meg fit into this faltering little world?

"You know we're going to have a great time, and you'll be with me the whole weekend. Do you know how long a weekend is?"

"It's two days, and a week is five days," Kimble flatly offered.

"Daddy is away now, but you'll see him very soon."

Kimble took off her barrette and stuck the end in her mouth.

"I notice you and your dad are real pals. Maybe we could be pals too. Not in the same way, of course, but…"

Kimble's eyes welled up. She began to whine, to rock back and forth within the confines of her shoulder harness.

In the bathroom at a Texaco station off the Palisades, Meg showed Kimble the Little Mermaid overnight bag and invited her to open it. She asked Kimble if she liked the jeans and T-shirts inside.

"I like my dress."

"Your dress is beautiful, but this is what people wear in the country. Don't you want to be a country girl?"

Kimble shook her head vigorously. Her lower lip began to quiver; two bright flares appeared over her pale cheeks.

It was imperative that Kimble cooperate, but Meg did not want to contradict or discipline her. For an instant she thought of calling Charlotte, who would be more than happy to share her gained wisdom. Then she thought better of it. This was not the moment to hear her mother invoke the model child Meg had been. The implied contrast between Meg's childhood and current behavior toward Charlotte would not benefit the moment.

Reluctant to have Kimble see her at a loss, Meg suddenly bit the price tag off the stiff new overalls. Kimble stared, fascinated by this wanton disregard of civility. Tentatively she began to giggle.

"What, your daddy uses scissors?"

Kimble gawked. Her smile flickered. Picking up the lost momentum, Meg swiftly bit the tags off the T-shirts, the sandals, the rain slicker. Kimble burst into her laugh, the laugh of Seal Island. Grateful to have been delivered, Meg remained patient while Kimble went on beyond all proportion.

Finally they tried on the new clothes. Every gesture, every new layer bared, was a revelation to Meg, who had not seen a toddler's body in many years. The loose, unmuscled skin of Kimble's round chest; her tiny, fat toes, nails still streaked with glitter polish ("See?" asked Kimble, pointing to her toes); her mottled little thighs beneath the sagging bluebird-patterned underpants—all were distant, familiar, achingly exotic placed amid this annual ride to Sullivan County.

Meg pointed to Kimble's underpants. "I bet we'll see birds just like those."

Kimble covered herself with both hands and swayed back and forth. Meg presented the jeans, rolled down for Kimble to step into. Staring dreamily ahead, Kimble, accommodating as a well-maintained machine, lifted each leg in turn. As Meg pulled the jeans up, Kimble began to sing a song about a porcupine. Meg had only so much as touch the T-shirt inside the Little Mermaid bag, and Kimble lifted her arms above her head. Her compliance left Meg speechless. Were Kimble an adult, Meg would have marveled at how she carried on while she could so easily have been paralyzed with anticipated remorse.

∞   ∞   ∞

Two days later, traveling east on Route 17, Meg and Kimble reviewed the events of the crafts fair. For Meg it had been a big success. She had sold considerably more fertility vessels than usual. Although she told customers Kimble was not her daughter, they seemed determined to believe the focused energy of Meg's work had brought the little girl into being. Most of the women drawn to the fertility goddesses in Meg's booth were in their mid or late thirties, maybe early forties, and had all tried for some time to conceive. To Meg, they seemed remarkably unmindful of the role of sperm in producing a fetus. Their ovaries had been tested, engineered, and tampered with, and their faith was flagging. After buying a pot or two, these women speculated with Meg about the source of their infertility—too many abortions in their twenties, too many years on the pill, faulty IUDs, a couple of suspicious drug trips back in "those years." Never did their partner's sperm seem to play a part.

Rather, these savvy, middle-aged women were poised to once again embrace the stork. So when they saw Kimble beside Meg it was irrelevant that Meg had not conceived her; she was simply a desirable little girl who had somehow wafted into the realm of the woman who threw pots in the shape of fertility goddesses.

Kimble seemed also to have had a successful weekend. She made friends with Sammy, the son of a watercolorist Meg had known for years. Sammy's 14-year-old sister had taken the two of them on a tour of the booths and to play with her Welsh corgi near a compost bin at the edge of the fairgrounds. Best of all, as Meg was driving to their small motel off the interstate a deer stopped frozen in the path of their headlights. Kimble had pushed her face to the windshield. When she pressed her palm against the dashboard the deer cantered off, leaving behind a testament to Meg's credibility.

Giddy with triumph, Meg began the review. The difference between a child and an adult, she reasoned, was term of memory. With an adult, she would muse over happy memories of the distant past; with a child, yesterday was the distant past. "Remember Sammy?"

"Yes," Kimble whispered.

"He was a nice little boy. Did you like him?"

"Yes. Except he spit."

"Disgusting, huh?"

"Yes. Girls don't spit."

"Girls are highly evolved."

"I know." Kimble managed a disaffected tone.

"And remember the Magic Fingers? You liked those, didn't you?"

"I did it three times," said Kimble. "Three different quarters. Grandma Shirl always has quarters. For the slot machines."

"I'm taking you to Grandma Shirl's now, as a matter of fact."

"Uh-*uh*. She's gambling. She won't see me till...uh, I forget."

Meg said nothing. Honey had neglected to tell her the grandmother would not be back on Sunday night.

"I want to see Daddy," whined Kimble.

Suddenly, from nowhere, Meg longed for a session of self-communion, the luxury to daydream, all the usual ways she nurtured herself deep within the privacy of her independence. With alarming swiftness she felt it necessary that her tour within a child's world now draw to a close. It was for just this feeling Meg had decided not to have children; in a world of serene women she was the only one in danger of cracking from the strain of deferring to a child's perspective. After a long session with a child, Meg would glance into a mirror to find herself preternaturally aged. Now, catching her reflection in the sideview mirror of the minivan, she flinched at the sight of her stiff mouth.

Kimble was crying. Her mouth had dropped open, emitting no sound except one sharp intake of breath—a gasp she choked on—and then she pitched forth a shriek that announced the end of any good faith between them. Meg pulled the van over to the shoulder. Kimble's whole body shook. With each fresh sob she seemed to peer into a new dimension of misery. By all appearances, she had taken this moment to unveil a hidden wretchedness in the world. Meg reached over to touch her hair, and new spate of wailing began. Kimble pounded at her knees. "Daddy!" Her tone was at first a protest, then an entreaty, then a series of hiccups bouncing in her chest.

"We're going to your daddy," said Meg. "Right now. That's where we're going."

All the way back to Manhattan, Kimble slept. When they

hit a pothole, she momentarily jolted awake. "Hi, Meg," she said, at once somnolent and acutely oriented, in the way of children whose immediate surroundings are everything.

∞   ∞   ∞

Barry was packed in ice. Thick curtains were drawn, the overhead lights were out, and there was only a dull square of radiance from the mini TV attached to the side rail of the bed—that, and the distant corridor fluorescence. He was attached to an IV drip; his eyes open, focused on the ceiling. "It's the shake-and-bake drug."

"Oh," said Meg. While Kimble had been chasing the little Welsh corgi and Meg selling her whimsical pots, they had found out it was crypto. Cryptococcalmeningitis—the major symptom of which was said to be headaches of unimaginable intensity. The hospital had started a course of amphotericin, a drug that wreaked havoc on the body's thermostat. "How's your head?"

"Better. The drug's killing me. Drugs kill. I been sayin' that for years." His voice was strong, but he winced as he spoke.

"Kimble's visiting at the nurse's station. Where she's being royally fussed over, I might add. Should I get her?"

Even though Barry was surrounded by ice, his forehead was filmed over with sweat. "Look," he said, then paused.

Meg wanted to take his hand but decided against it. Within the artificial bounds of her REACH relationships, she had honed her judgments over time. She knew signals. She leaned closer.

"Look, I've timed this thing so far. She sees me when it's gonna make her happy. Otherwise, she sees Shirl or Honey. Or now you. That's the way it's been."

"It's not that simple, Barry. You know I can't keep Kimble. Your mother-in-law went off gambling, but nobody knows where. We have to find her right away. REACH is going to take Kimble away from me, and if we don't find Shirley, they're going to have to call the city and put her in foster care."

"The social worker from downstairs was up here," said Barry. It took some time for him to get the words out. "She'd been talkin' to someone at So-You-Finally-Reached-Over-Here. She had a real bug up her ass about Kimble, so I told her I just got a call from Shirl and that Shirl was on her way over to your house to pick up Kimble. Not such a stretch. Shirl'll be back. It's just a matter of when."

Meg started to ask Barry what assurances he could give her that Shirley Marzola would be back within the next couple of days, but Barry shuddered with a frightening intensity and closed his eyes. His lids were gray, dusted with patchy scales. His cheeks were pallid and sunken, a look Meg knew foretold either imminent death or phenomenal recovery, depending upon nothing at all.

3

"How was your weekend?" asked Charlotte over the phone before 9 the next morning. Meg had only picked up because she thought it might be Tina from REACH—or Honey, or the grandmother, or Barry himself.

"Oh, God. Yes, fine. It went well."

"Good!" cheered Charlotte. From her mother's tone, Meg might have just managed to round the block on her first two-wheeler. Then came the sound of Charlotte sipping coffee. She was settling in.

"Listen, I'll have to call you back."

"All right." She did not say good-bye. "I thought next time we could go to Tavern on the Green, courtesy of the surprise little premium I told you about."

"OK, fine. Do you mind if I call you back?" Meg repeated. But then, "How are you?"

"I'm fine. Getting ready for the trip. There's a million things to do. I feel like I'm going to another planet." Charlotte made these breezy remarks in a depressed tone of voice.

"I'm sure you'll pull it together," Meg said absently.

"I'm glad you did well over the weekend. I'd love to see the new pots."

"You'll have to come over before you leave."

"Actually, I'm going to be in your neighborhood today. That little shop you told me about is putting new locks on my luggage."

"Today's not so good, I'm afraid. I have a little girl with me."

"Oh? Whose?"

"You know, the client I told you about."

"Oh yes, the *client*. I won't ask you why. I just hope it's legal," Charlotte chuckled. In Meg's opinion, chuckles did not exist in the nature of human sounds. They were little contrivances people manufactured when they were angry but wanted to sound wry.

The ring of the phone had woken Kimble. She tiptoed around the plaster partition that marked off Meg's bedroom. She was wearing one of Meg's T-shirts. A sleep fold was inscribed into her left cheek, and her cottony hair inclined toward several invisible electric currents. "Is that Daddy?"

"Daddy's sleeping now," Meg told Kimble. "We'll talk to him later."

"Meg? Are you there? Is that her?"

Meg wanted to hurry Charlotte off the phone. She felt badly that Kimble would know she was not speaking to someone from her own tiny inner circle, the only tangible shape in her life.

"Meg...whose child *is* this, anyway?"

"Mother, there's a lot happening here at once. I'll call you back later."

"No hurry," her mother said in the same chirpy tone Meg's childhood "Chatty Cathy" had emitted every time her string was pulled, whether she was being tucked into her cradle or bashed over her head.

∞   ∞   ∞

At 10:15, shortly after the REACH offices opened, Meg dropped Kimble off at the children's basement playroom. Several children were already there, drinking juice and arguing over the pieces of a jigsaw puzzle. Some children were positive. Others were negative but had sick parents in Group Services or at appointments upstairs.

Kimble hung back. Sensing Meg was about to abandon her, her jaw began to work up and down as her face grew hot with color. Meg stepped backward. She remembered how terror could get trapped in the throat, then mount as it recognized the danger of never being released. She waited. When Kimble's wail finally burst forth, a siren of present and projected misery, Meg was amazed that the children with their juice and their puzzle pieces did not even look up. She heard one say to another, "You bitchhead, gimme that back."

Kimble's chest heaved. She gasped for breath. She began to tug at the country clothes she wore, the jeans and T-shirt Meg had bought her. She bunched a section of cotton T-shirt in her fist and stretched it out as far as it would go, then let it spring back. She did this over and over. When she saw she did not have the strength to tear the shirt, she threw herself to the floor, grabbed a wooden block from a bridge-building set, and pounded it against the carpet. When it became clear to her this would have no destructive effect, she flung her arm against a chair leg, withdrew from the stinging pain, then did it again. Her renewed sobs took on an added tone, an overlay of pure accusation.

The staff member in charge of the children, a young man in his twenties with a rhinestone string dangling from his ear, shrugged at Meg, silently asking her to cue his instructions. She smiled wanly and lifted her open hand in the air.

When the heaves grew weaker, Meg sat down beside Kimble. She did not touch her. Meg was surprised at how deeply *she* shook inside.

"Kimmy, I know how you feel. I know how hard it is for you that your daddy's sick. I wish I could make him better for you." Meg struggled to keep her voice even. "I really, truly do."

One more wail, immensely sorrowful, then nothing. Silence.

"This is what's happening. I'm going to leave you with Ray over there and these children to play. This will be for a very short while—say, two hours, three at the most. You can ask Ray what time it is as much as you'd like. Ray is a nice man, and it's his job to take care of children whose parents are sick like your daddy. There are a lot of games and books here, and later a clown is coming. I'm going to see your daddy. I really wish I could bring you with me, but the hospital doesn't allow children. But I'll bring a message from your daddy. Is there anything you'd like me to tell him?"

Kimble flipped over on her back. She stared through swollen eyes at a mobile that was hanging from the light fixture. Finally she said, "To come get me." She began to cry again and turned back over on her stomach so Meg could not see her.

Meg rubbed Kimble's back for several minutes. Then she signaled to Ray, who came over with a paddleball. Kimble was asleep.

∞   ∞   ∞

Barry was no longer packed in ice. They had stopped the amphotericin. Now there was a morphine drip, new as of this morning, according to the chart at the end of the bed.

"Stoned again," Barry said. "Ya know how many times I was detoxed in the hospital? Pretty funny, huh? So, did you see? Here's my inventory: crypto, pleurisy, microsporidiosis—or CMV colitis, they can't make up their minds—herpes again, and, hey, the heartbreak of psoriasis."

"Jesus," said Meg.

"How's my little Kimmy? They told me she's not gonna get it. They said it was clear sailin'. You know these things...whaddya think? Think she's not gonna get it?"

"If she hasn't seroconverted by now, she won't," Meg said with an air of aplomb she heard and detested. "You shouldn't worry."

"So, it's a miracle, huh? Anita shoulda lived long enough to see the miracle. Anita was a nun—I ever tell you that? Yeah, I lured her from the convent, no kiddin'. I actually met her in NA. She came with some little runaway, you know, to give her support, and that was the beginning. She woulda left the convent anyway; she never shoulda been there. But there was a history there I won't go into. Anyway, Kimmy was tested for the last time when Anita was practically gone. I told her the truth; just like you said, negative now will stay negative. But Anita didn't believe me: She thought I was lyin' to make her die all right. She didn't, though. She died feelin' like she shoulda never lived."

"That's terrible," said Meg. Oddly, the morphine was having anything but a sedative effect. She made a mental note to speak to the nurse.

"Would ya mind turning me over?" Barry asked. "I don't wanna bug the nurses. They got their hands full on this floor. You notice? Every door's got a yellow sign. Yellow-and-black signs just like when I used to go hunting upstate, posted No Trespassing."

"I guess we can just turn you on this side," Meg said. She didn't want to disturb the IV drip. Like rolling dough with the heels of her hands, she pushed him onto his right side. Despite her gentle touch, Barry moaned. The blue hospital gown parted in the back. Diapers.

"How's that?"

"Yeah, better, thanks. I can usually stand it this way about 15 minutes, then I gotta go back. They were supposed to get me one of those egg-crate things, ya know the ones? But they got their hands full. You think you can move me back before you go?"

"Of course." Meg dragged a chair over to the other side of the bed so she could face Barry.

"So how's Kimmy? I asked you already, but I don't really wanna hear, if ya know what I mean."

"She's fine. I left her at REACH." Meg glanced at her watch. "They have a clown coming about now."

"Oh, that's great," said Barry. His voice had abandoned its gangster inflection. "That's really great," he repeated.

"Barry, I actually came to talk about Kimmy. I know that when you contacted REACH, one thing that was on your mind was making arrangements for her."

Barry looked directly at Meg. "Anyone who's put off joinin' the real world for as long as I have ain't exactly gonna make a chart of his kid's every move for after he dies. Ya know what I mean?"

Meg was silent. She watched the IV drip.

"Ya know what it's like? It's like if I face this thing, if I say what should happen to Kimmy, if I put it down on paper or somethin', that's like my death knell."

Meg wanted to listen with her whole self. Instead, she got caught on how Barry had insinuated the redoubtable phrase "death knell" into his usual street talk.

"So, it's hard for me," Barry went on. "But I guess I should be used to hard by now."

Meg touched his shoulder, rubbed his arm. His eyes filled with tears.

"I don't know what to do. Shirl can't take her. She says she wants her one moment, then says she can't do it the next. Honey once said she'd take her, but she didn't mean it. What am I gonna do?"

"There are some good people in the foster care system today," said Meg. "People who will take good care of Kimmy and...try to adopt her."

"I heard there're gays tryin' to adopt. I know I shouldn't make a big deal, you from REACH and all. But I don't want that."

Involuntarily, Meg withdrew her hand. It hovered for a moment between her side and Barry's arm.

"That was bad, huh? I'm just a dyed-in-the-wool bigot."

"And I'm just a dyed-in-the wool dyke," said Meg.

"So, hey, at least we're both dyed in the wool, ya know?" He did not skip a beat.

Meg smiled. She rested her hand again on Barry's arm. "What about Kimmy?"

"Kimmy gets everything I have. Bring around someone an' I'll write it down. All I ask is she don't go to Shirl. There's bad history there, like I said. I'd rather have her go to a good stranger than to Shirl. Can I put that in writing too?"

"I'm not sure. I'll have to get back to you on that."

Barry opened his mouth to say something. As he did the air between them filled with a foul odor. Meg tried to keep her gaze steady, but Barry, unable to move, scanned up and down the baseboards with his eyes. His expression, like an infant's, fled from the edge of revelation to pure venom in a split second. "Get *outta* here," he commanded.

Meg got up. "Shall I turn you?"

"Out!" he yelled, and Meg stepped quickly out of the room and down the corridor. She stopped at the nurse's station to explain what had happened in Barry's room—as if the hospital room itself had been responsible for Barry's accident.

Inside the empty elevator she was confronted with the inexorable truth that there was not a single thing she could do for Barry once his essential grace had been violated. She began to cry, to bawl like Kimble really, except that rather than fall into a hollow from which she would have to be rescued, she walked through the lobby and onto the street, one of countless New York streets where the tears of adults go unnoticed.

4

On Saturday mornings Meg usually went running along West Street. Then she had breakfast at her diner, where specials in faded lettering had for years hung on the quilted aluminum walls. There she read the *Times* and listened to veteran hookers forcing gems of worldly wisdom upon teenage runaways. This Saturday morning, however, Meg was in her kitchen area, pouring milk into a bowl of Rice Krispies. She was immured in a sense of deprivation and had no trouble acknowledging it to herself. Kimble was awake but in bed, talking to Roller Queen, a doll wearing skates, stiff orange ringlets, and nothing else.

Last Monday Meg had called Honey, who had given her Shirl's number. For days the phone there had gone unanswered by person or machine. Meg had driven to Barry's Washington Heights building. Honey had the key to his apartment and let Meg in to gather some of Kimble's clothes and toys. Honey had whistled and hummed as she strode down the hall but had not offered to take Kimble. Meg had intended to ask, then firmly changed her mind. Now she suffered. Both Kimble's voice (content and enchanted with itself) and the crackling from the cereal bowl were pleasing sounds but did not begin to make up for the endorphin rush of an early-morning run, for Meg's customary Saturday hour to savor the mundane.

"Rice Krispies!" she called out. Meg had discovered that for a child, intonation could alter reality. The likes of Rice Krispies and tepid baths could be turned into sensual pleasures of the highest order, if properly heralded. Meg loved this about Kimble, but at the same time wondered when she would wise up.

Kimble emerged from behind one of the several drywall partitions in Meg's loft. She held Roller Queen by her plastic skates.

"Now, how would you feel if someone held *you* by your feet?"

"Good. I'd like it."

"It would be different, wouldn't it? Do you like Rice Krispies?" Rice Krispies was the only cereal Meg had in the house.

"Yes. So does Roller Queen. Except she doesn't eat as much as me."

"Really? With all that skating? She must have a slow metabolism."

"No. She's not a slow modalsome. She's just not a pig."

"Well, I guess it's all right if she eats from your bowl, then. OK?"

"OK." Kimble climbed onto the high stool at the slab stone countertop where Meg ate. Also on the countertop was a glazed, russet-colored fruit bowl, Meg's first pot. It was filled with nectarines and bananas. "Can I have a 'nana?"

"Of course." Meg sat across from Kimble and Roller Queen, who was propped on Kimble's lap and who repeatedly fell forward and knocked her head against the cereal bowl. Meg peeled half a banana and reached across to slice it into Kimble's bowl. She ate the rest of the banana while Kimble stared at her.

"Why do you live here all by yourself?"

"Does that seem strange to you? Your daddy lives alone."

"He lives with me!"

Meg put two fingers to her lips and rocked slightly, as if considering a subtle observation by Kimble. In truth, the little girl had found her out, had shamed her. Meg was one of those people who did not regard children as verifiably human. "That's true. I meant he doesn't live with another adult."

"But there are other adults in the *hos*-pit-al. No children, just adults. They hate children."

"No, they don't. They just don't want a lot of noise where sick people are trying to get well." Meg could not believe she had introduced the concept of *well*.

"I don't make noises."

"That's true, you really don't. Sometimes strict rules are made because of the bad behavior of a few." (*You sanctimonious asshole,* Meg said to herself.)

"Roller Queen's not hungry at all today. So I get more."

"That's fine. And then I'm going to help you get dressed. We're going out. To an *appointment.*" Along with elevating the mundane through excited inflections, Meg had discovered that if she made certain words sound official, she could nudge Kimble into a reverent silence.

∞   ∞   ∞

Like a storefront palm reader, Libby Zindel was always available to her customers. Party clowns and manicurists might have clients, but Libby had customers, and she loved to say so. "You'll buy goods and services from me," she had said. "You'll buy my ear, my time, my infinite goodwill. And once a year I sell Girl Scout cookies for my granddaughter."

"That's the exact opposite of the point of the cookie drive," Meg had startled herself by saying. "They're supposed to learn self-reliance. They're supposed to bask in their first capitalist success."

"Every great capitalist has a blind partner," Libby had defended.

After a few sessions with Libby, Meg saw why the term *client* would never do. "Can we really call you a therapist?" Meg asked, daring to extend herself into Libby's unbounded reach.

"Let's not."

"What, then?"

"The good mother."

"*Please.*"

Still, Meg had returned. They had regularly scheduled twice-weekly appointments, but Libby also let it be known she might be available for impromptu sessions should the need arise. The need had arisen this week, and Meg had called Libby late the night before. They had scheduled their appointment for 11 o'clock that morning. "Give me some peace with my bagel," Libby had said. Meg had understood.

At 11 o'clock sharp Libby opened the door to her apartment on West End Avenue. She wore a taupe cashmere sweater, a gray flannel skirt, high heels, and several bangles. She wore silver-and-onyx earrings, rouge, and crimson lipstick. Eyebrow pencil. "I like to look like a million bucks while I get sucked into the abyss with my customers," she had once said.

When Libby took a step into the vestibule, Kimble backed

up. The vividness of Libby's appearance shocked Kimble, who seemed to experience her own airy looks as did others: as evidence of her fragile domination over gravity.

Libby kneeled down. "Hello, Kimble. I'm so glad you could come today."

Kimble began to cry.

"Too many people. It's a constant changing of the guards for her."

Now Kimble backed up into the door across the hall.

"Come on, Kimmy. This is Libby. I told you we were coming to visit Libby."

"I've got cookies inside, Kimmy. Pepperidge Farm Milanos."

"Oh great, cookies. I bet you'd love some cookies."

"No. Ho Ho's."

Meg made a face. "We have to upgrade your taste in junk food."

"Daddy's Ho Ho's!"

"OK," said Libby. "I'm going to run downstairs to get you some Ho Ho's. You go inside with Meg now."

"The good mother," remarked Meg.

Libby put on a light coat and left the apartment. Meg walked in with Kimble. The sound of a vacuum cleaner came from another room. Meg had never been alone in Libby's apartment, but she was not particularly curious. She already knew that Libby had painted the framed watercolors. She knew the faux finish on the fireplace had been payment in barter from a customer who made his living marbleizing. Libby even had one of Meg's pots, which she had asked for rather than payment for a week's sessions. ("Oh, *money* again," she had declared. "Can't we be a *little* more creative?")

"Daddy's Ho Ho's," Kimble chanted to herself, no longer crying.

"On their way, Little Princess. Are you going to show Libby Roller Queen?"

"No. She's naked."

"Libby likes naked dolls."

"No, she doesn't. She's old."

"Please don't say that when Libby gets back."

"Why?"

"It's not polite."

Before long came the sound of the inner and outer elevator doors opening. Libby walked into the unlocked apartment. She was carrying a paper bag and emptied its contents on the sideboard in her foyer. There were two packages of Ho Ho's, three of Ring-Dings, and one each of Twinkies and Sno Balls.

"Wow!" said Meg.

"Wow!" imitated Kimble. "Daddy's food."

Pleased with herself, Libby looked at Meg.

"I'm opening it, OK?" asked Kimble, and began to tear a Ho Ho package with her teeth.

"She learned that from me," said Meg.

Kimble took a big bite and swallowed it after barely three chews. Then she asked Libby, "Why are you old?"

"So I can say whatever I want *when*ever I want," answered Libby. Then, as an afterthought: "Just like you."

Meg, silent during this exchange, could not look at Libby. For months she had scrupulously avoided any reference to Libby's age. Anytime her divulgences in Libby's consultation room led to her own fear of old age and death, she had censored herself. Feckless Kimble had now violated months of discreet behavior. Worse, she had drawn from Libby a perfectly sensible response, one that showed up Meg's true cowardice.

"I think Libby's going to have you eat those in another room," prodded Meg.

"Yes. Elena, could you come out here, please?"

Libby's cleaning woman came out from the dining room.

"This is Kimble. Remember, I told you about Kimble?"

"Yes? Oh, good."

"Can you watch her for a while? Kimble, would you mind going with Elena? You can help her clean, or you can eat, or you can look at my bird feeder out back. Anything you want."

Elena smiled broadly and held out her hand. Kimble immediately grasped hold.

"So what're you going to do?"

"Jesus, Libby, let me cross my legs, will you?" Meg had sunk back into Libby's huge blue recliner.

"There's no time to waste, and you know it."

"I don't know what I'm going to do. That's why I'm here."

Libby leaned forward, the shine on her leather high heels glistening in the noon light. "You know, I, myself, try to avoid these pivotal moments in life. These moments in which a decision must be made and the decision has consequences. But you can't run from the fact that you have a major decision before you. And you are prepared to make it, because you have participated in the evolution of circumstances thus far." Libby virtually sang out the word *thus*. She smiled coyly.

This was how it was with Libby and Meg. Real emotion embarrassed them. They knew it was their business to pursue its expression, but they could only back into real emotion through ironic introductions. "I'm not so sure. I think I tried to avoid circumstances, as usual. It's not my fault the grandmother disappeared and there's no one else."

"There's someone else. There's always someone else."

"Oh, come on, Libby. How can I let her go to an agency? I can break my back to get her into one of the good ones, Leake and Watts, but those places have waiting lists. And how many changes can she *stand*? For little kids, too many changes have consequences."

Libby leaned back to light a cigarette. She was wearing an acupuncture needle in her ear and a nicotine patch under her bra, and she still smoked half a pack of cigarettes a day. "What do you think your mother would say?"

"Oh, shit, do I have to tell her?"

Libby smiled. Her eyes twinkled.

"I haven't made any decisions yet."

Libby took a long drag on the cigarette and snuffed it out. "I think you'd be a wonderful mother, Meg," she said. "I think you are going to save that little girl's life, and I know you have the courage to do it."

Meg was silent. She breathed thick, wobbly breaths. She stared at some papers on Libby's desk across the room. It was useless; the tears could not be held back. The suddenness of her crying frightened her, made her cry more. Her chest swelled, her nose ran. "What kind of a fuckin' therapist's office has no Kleenex?" she spluttered. The bridge of her nose throbbed.

Libby took a handkerchief from the pocket of her flannel skirt.

"This is *used!*" exclaimed Meg.

"So?" asked Libby, wide-eyed.

They burst out laughing. Then Meg was quiet. Amazingly, Libby honored her silence. Deep inside her body, Meg filled up with the singular sense of calm that follows such outbursts. She was almost sleepy.

"What am I going to do when I have to be alone? How am I going to go running? What if I forgot to get milk for the morning and it's the middle of the night and 10 degrees out?"

"You have within you an untold reserve of solutions," said Libby.

"Yeah, right."

Libby withdrew into her leather armchair. She hugged a kilim pillow to her chest. "So when're you gonna tell Mom?" The natural blush of her cheeks flared out around the rouge— two complementary hues of the same tone, demonstrating that Libby might actually be a woman of considered choices.

While Barry Toffler lay dying barely five yards away, Meg played Go Fish with his daughter Kimble. They were in the corridor just outside his room. Visiting hours had not begun, but the nurses tolerated their presence. Kimble sat on the cracked leather seat of a St. Luke's wheelchair. She appeared particularly comfortable. Meg wondered if, for her, the wheelchair was an overgrown stroller, proof that people of all ages periodically fell into the care of others. They played on a dinner tray that Meg had rolled up to the wheelchair. Kimble was flushed. Whenever Meg asked her for a card not in her hand, she commanded "Go Fish!" Her tone vibrated with the overcharged exultation of the utterly powerless. Meg noticed she was beginning to lose the frangible look of the day they met. She would never be a robust child, but Meg could now imagine an axis to her, a bit of something structural toward which experience might reasonably gravitate.

Kimble knew the purpose of their visit. Meg had told her she might today be saying good-bye to her father. It had fallen to Meg to tell Kimble this. In the van on the way up to St. Luke's she had broken out in a sweat. Earlier, she had wanted to call Tina at REACH to ask for advice, but this was impossible. For the first time in her seven years of volunteering, she had lied to the REACH office. More than a week before, she had told Tina that Shirley Marzola had returned to pick up Kimble. There had been some emergency, Meg had explained, with a friend on Long Island, but Kimble was back with her grandmother now. This had merely been a corroboration of Barry's story to the hospital social worker. Tina had been pleased, had said she would work with St. Luke's social service to help transfer legal guardianship to Shirley Marzola. If Tina had known Shirl was not even in town, she would most certainly have arranged for short-term placement for the little girl. At REACH, crises rippled outward. Small ones drifted into larger ones. Weary from seven years of stopgap problem-solving, Meg had decided to lie, to coast along the lie for as long as it held.

Hospitals were much in Meg's life. Even when her clients had large and concerned families, Meg was often included in an inner circle. She had rotated with four of Jerry's friends in spending the night on a cot next to his bed. The nurses at NYU had allowed this. In Jerry's last days they had encouraged it. By the time Meg arrived with her duffel bag, a cot had already been made up with a frayed, starched sheet and a white thermal blanket. Its taut surface was a cold welcome. Jerry had usually slept through the night, while Meg jolted awake each time a nurse entered to check his IV or empty his catheter bag, the bag of bloody urine that had become a part of Jerry. At the end, not an hour had passed in which urine or sputum or vomit did not enter into their contract together, and rarely did they miss a chance to use it as a marker of their mighty friendship. "Oh, how *bonding*," Jerry would say after he spat up bile into the curved little tray Meg held under his chin. Meg would smooth back his hair, would rest her palm on the tacky skin of his forehead.

One bright morning, he woke before she did. He had heard her stir but was unable to turn his head in her direction. "Would her lady like champagne with breakfast this morning? We made it through another night."

"*You* did," Meg had rejoined. His irreverence had long since cued her responses; nothing was off-limits. Meg had risen slowly. She had felt as if microscopic insects were running across her eyes. The small of her back had ached. Jerry's roommate was in the bathroom, so Meg had gone into the hall to brush her teeth. Perfectly healthy, she had shuffled down the hospital corridor in her slippers. By the time she had returned, three nurses were aspirating Jerry. She had backed out of the room. She had sat in a wheelchair in the hall until Fran, Jerry's favorite morning nurse, came out and shook her head.

Now Kimble sat in another wheelchair in a shabbier corridor. She shot up from the chair, suddenly full of pride as she recognized her superior card hand. Meg wanted to be anywhere but at this hospital. Whatever was next in life, she decided, she was through nosing up to death.

"Go Fish, you bitch, go fish!"

"Kimble. That is absolutely, under no circumstances, allowed."

"They say it at REACH," claimed Kimble.

"They don't say it near me. And neither will you."

Kimble stopped talking. Instead she forced four unpronounced syllables from her throat, a tuneless bar breathed to the rhythm of "Go fish, you bitch."

Meg knew that she must let this intransigence pass. She was surprised at how difficult it was for her to do this. She was overtaken by a need to triumph over this child, to show her that her little machinations would not be tolerated. Heartily insulted by a four-and-a-half-year-old, she could not believe how wounded she felt. It was all she could do not to pout, not to punish Kimble by throwing down her hand and walking away from their game.

Kimble kept right on humming. Meg grew steely inside. An aide paused beside them. She had come from Barry's room. She carried two lunch trays, one whose food remained untouched. "He wants to see you," she said. Unable to point, she jabbed her elbow in Kimble's direction.

"Just her?" Meg asked.

"That's all he said," the aide answered. Meg nodded. She watched a square of strawberry Jell-O shimmy in response to the aide's labored breaths.

Kimble stopped humming her taunting notes. Her face went white. Her ethereal, not-quite-there presence returned. She was like a vision someone had not finished conjuring.

"Go on, sweetie," said Meg. "I'll wait here."

Kimble rose. Meg had made sure she wore the imitation Laura Ashley today. Now Kimble smoothed out the skirt. Her fingers, rosy at the joints, plied together to make a flat surface that would tame the unruly folds of the dress. Her fingers were too small to caress, too virtuous to dawdle. She directed them over her skirt with a great sense of purpose. She smoothed and smoothed, and when her eyes grew vacant it was because all other voluntary functions had failed her. Meg had to lay a hand on her arm.

"Go now, sweetie. You look beautiful. Your daddy will love how you look."

Kimble walked toward Barry's room. With her flyaway blond hair drifting off her pink neck, she was little more than a toddler taking her first reluctant steps into the ever gravid world. She leaned slightly to the right, drawn there by the weight of Roller Queen—dressed for the occasion in a felt skirt—dangling in her grasp.

As soon as Meg saw the backs of Kimble's patent leather shoes disappear, she got up and walked down the corridor. Along the way she glanced inside all the doors. Eight years of visiting clients in the hospital had not rid her of this prurient habit. The only difference between now and her first year of volunteering was that now the diseases her own body had eluded seemed closer, not in the sense of lurking threats but as parts of a grand inevitability. Meg no longer recoiled from the world of the ill, but she did not understand what drove her to enter it time and again. Certainly she did not know why she continued to look into the open rooms. For the second time that day she resolved she would have no more of hospitals.

Meg took the elevator to the lobby, stood in front of an overhead TV tuned to a soap opera, reflected in an obligatory way on the program's inanity, then went quickly upstairs again. She peeked into Barry's room to let him know she was in the corridor. Kimble sat on a chair next to him, her head resting on Barry's bed. Her head was turned toward his bare feet, which stuck out from the hospital blanket. Kimble did not look at the feet, scaly from psoriasis, but at Roller Queen, whose opinion she seemed intent upon. Barry was rigidly propped on two pillows in fresh cases, his hand laying on Kimble's head. He coiled a strand of her hair around his finger. His own hair had been painstakingly combed. Over his hospital gown he wore a bow tie with outlandish fluorescent spots. Now he spoke to Meg. "I feel real good today," he announced. Where the timbre of his voice might have been, there was only the vibration produced by his unfathomable weakness. He looked like a dead man. Meg retreated.

Five minutes later Kimble came out. The spotted bow tie dangled from Roller Queen's neck. "He says you're supposed to tell me how to be from now on," she relayed. "If you want, he says you could."

5

Several times over the past few months, after she had potted all day long with no company but a string of WBAI guests, Meg had been overtaken by an urge to track down Sarina. Finding Sarina Willard would not be hard; Meg knew she had moved to a small farm in southern Vermont, freelanced as a package designer, tapped maple trees for syrup, and was largely kept by Leah Bender, heiress to a small fortune in the world's first line of organic cosmetics. As Meg had heard it, Sarina habitually clarified for people that she had fallen in love with Leah thinking she was merely another Hunter College MSW student. She had no idea Leah would drop out of the program when it began to bog her down, would purchase a Vermont farm (Sarina's dream) for cash. Meg had heard from several sources that they seemed solid together, but she had never believed it. During these powerful yearnings to call Sarina, Meg convinced herself that the relationship had grown loveless, that Leah's fortune held Sarina hostage. She imagined her call as a heroic rescue. She imagined a sublime reunion that dispensed with the reality of their final months together, months in which Meg had hounded Sarina with her fears of being abandoned. When Sarina eventually walked out, she had left no forwarding address. They had not spoken since, had not had what Meg's friends called "closure." This lack of closure, her friends claimed, accounted for Meg's recurring temptation to call Sarina. They always offered the same advice: Have an affair.

Of course, Meg had had affairs. Much later, when she had finally disclaimed her overwrought intimacy with Sarina—their promise to die together—when she had come to see their late-night vows as juvenile little melodramas, when at last she knew that sex was not a matter of two bodies snuffing out their loss-es, when she had finally let the laundry dancing outside the neighbor's window enter into the meter of her lovemaking, then she had become someone who had affairs, someone who seduced. Yet scarcely a week had passed, at best a month, that her thoughts did not drift to Sarina.

This morning she did nothing but think about her. Barry Toffler had died in the middle of the night before. Kimble now slept under a Little Mermaid quilt on the futon in the back of the loft. Meg had no idea what would come next for either of them. She remembered that Sarina used to fantasize about Meg getting pregnant, about Meg as tranquil Madonna. The vividness of these fantasies had drawn Meg in, had enabled her to imagine the singular drive to have a child. It was this mem-ory that drove her to call. This time she did not want a friend to talk her out of it. She picked up the phone and dialed Putney information. Sarina still lived there.

"Hello!" This hale voice could only be bolstered by a trust fund.

"Hello. Is Sarina there, please?"

"She's out back. Who's calling?"

"Meg. An old friend."

Sarina might have told Leah everything about Meg; she might have told her nothing. Time and again this very inscrutability had piqued Meg's distrust.

"Just a minute. She's finally fixing the weed whacker."

How could Leah address Meg as if she had come pre-installed in their lives? How could she assume that Meg knew they had a weed whacker and that it required fixing? How could she presume that Meg agreed it was about time Sarina got to the weed whacker? Meg deplored this kind of narcissism, the kind that revealed itself within 15 seconds.

Soon came a rustling on the other end of the line. "Hello?" Sarina's greeting was tentative and sweet, as it had always been. How could Meg have ever distrusted the person who owned this voice?

"Sarina." Meg paused. Despite herself, she intended this word not as a greeting, but as a place to land. "Meg Krantz."

Stillness on the other end. Meg was not surprised. Did Sarina want to run? Did her weed whacker now urgently call? "Meg. How *are* you?"

"Well, what can I say? I don't remember how many years it's been. How many? Oh, you probably don't either. Lots, though." Jesus, thought Meg. She would have done better to script herself.

"Let's not date ourselves," Sarina said. "Are you all right?"

As if only terminal cancer could justify this call, thought Meg, remembering the reason for the distrust. "Yes, I'm fine. I've had my own business for a few years."

"I heard. Your pots. I heard it was going very well."

Meg and Sarina no longer had friends in common. She did not know how Sarina could have heard about her business. "Yes, pretty well. It's great to be my own boss. You're well?"

"Oh, I'm fine." Sarina had always affected a tone of dispensing with her own welfare—this, while mightily ensuring her future. "I think the country has ruined me for real society. I've grown dull-witted and eccentric."

"And happy?" Make her say it, thought Meg.

"Yes, I'm happy. How about you?"

"You know, I've gotten myself into a funny situation. Remember how before we ended I started volunteering for REACH? Well, I'm actually still there, and my client just died last night. But he has a daughter, Kimble, a little four-and-a-half-year-old."

"My God. She must be devastated."

"I haven't told her yet. She's asleep in the back, actually."

"Meg! She's with you?"

"There's no one else, really."

"Meg." Sarina lowered her voice. "Honey. Why did you call me?"

"I'm sorry. I don't know. It was indulgent. I'm really sorry, I don't know." Then, finally, "We never had closure." Meg could not believe she had said this. Some uncontrollable something rose in her throat, laughter by all rights, but sobbing when it emerged.

"Don't you think you're just nervous because you don't know what to do?"

"Yes. I guess that's it. I think I'm in over my head here."

"Take her out to breakfast. Order her pancakes. Tell her gently. You'll do fine."

"Her life could be horrible."

"You won't let it be, Meg."

There was nothing more to say. Libby would have killed her if she had heard this conversation. Meg did what she always did when left undefended. She apologized for her existence. "I'm sorry I called. I don't know why I did. But thanks."

"Oh, Meg."

"Stay well."

"You *too*. You stay well."

"I intend to," said Meg. Just then she heard the rubber soles of Kimble's pajama feet sticking and popping along the path to the bathroom.

∞   ∞   ∞

The reception line at the Toffler funeral, held at Fanelli's Memorial Home in Astoria, consisted only of Shirley Marzola and a Fanelli employee, an at-large pallbearer with whom Shirley seemed to have struck up some kind of alliance. The general attendance had been scant. In addition to Honey, who had hastily put together the service, there was only Meg and a group of men and women whom Meg overheard using the special language of The Rooms. The organ music was provided by Fanelli's, as was the eulogist, a rumpled-looking priest from the church across the street. He had delivered such an uninspired summary of Barry's life that anyone might reasonably wonder why Barry had lived. The priest had made no mention of Kimble. Meg concluded this omission was at Shirley Marzola's behest.

Shirley had probably come to Barry's funeral only for Kimble's sake, but Kimble was not there. Meg had dropped her off at REACH, where Ray had arranged a special afternoon. Each time a parent died, the Jolly Players came to give a performance. The success of the performance depended entirely on the participation of one member of the audience. Each time a kindly wizard in a flowing robe went out among the oversize pillows that surrounded the stage, looked about in tense deliberation, then waved a sparkling magic wand over the head of the child whose parent had just died. The child then assumed the role of enchanted prince or princess, a lofty and undemanding role entirely cued by the benevolent wizard. Sitting at Barry's funeral, Meg had wondered how Kimble would react to the timing of her sudden ascent into stardom. She had not touched her Rice Krispies that morning and had walked into the entrance of REACH with great reluctance. At the threshold of the playroom she had refused to budge. Meg had carried her to Ray, who had cocked his head and looked at her silently, preparing to give her his full attention. His readiness was all Kimble needed to see. All at once she was loose-muscled in her anguish. She had virtually poured into his arms.

Meg and Shirley Marzola had met twice, very briefly. The first time was just last Tuesday at St. Luke's. Barry had fallen into a coma the morning after he had sat dazed in his spotted bow tie, his wasted and blue-veined hand on Kimble's head. After two weeks away, Shirley had finally returned to her Rego Park apartment. When Meg called, Shirley's "hello" had been delivered in a carefree lilt. She had known who Meg was right away. With startling ingenuousness, she had thanked Meg for taking over Kimble's care while she was in Atlantic City. She had planned to return right away, she claimed, but she had finally gotten herself a winning combination and had taken some of the girls to Palm Beach. "After all," she had concluded, "life is for living." But now she was home, she had acknowledged, and there was "all this. You can run, but you can't hide."

"Do you realize that Kimble came within a hair of being swept off into the foster system?" Meg had interrupted. "I had to lie to REACH, and Barry had to lie to the St. Luke's social worker. Barry is in a coma now. The social worker thinks Kimble is with you, and I bet she's been calling you. I'm afraid you have to decide immediately, Mrs. Marzola. Will you be Kimble's legal custodian, or should we make other arrangements?"

"Other arrangements! My God, what are other arrangements? Of course I'll take her! How could there ever be a question?"

Meg had kept her voice free of inflection. She had told Shirley Marzola to call the St. Luke's social worker and go over there to sign some papers. Then she had given Shirley the name of the coffee shop across from the hospital, where she would wait with Kimble.

Once again Meg had been struck by Kimble's compliance as she passed from one hand to another. At the coffee shop, she had finished her milkshake and, clutching Roller Queen by one skate blade, had let Shirley lead her outside. She had looked back at Meg, but her face had been expressionless. Distantly, Meg had wondered at what point in Kimble's childhood she might sense she was entitled to have feelings about the events that affected her in momentous ways.

Two days later, the day after Barry died, Shirley had called Meg to ask her if she wouldn't mind taking Kimble for a few hours. Then, shortly before Kimble was due back in Queens, Shirley had called again to say she had picked up some sort of a virus. Would it be too inconvenient for Meg to keep Kimble until she was better, maybe after the funeral?

At Fanelli's Memorial Home, Meg advanced to the front of the tiny reception line. Wordlessly, she extended her hand.

Shirley Marzola grabbed the arm of the Fanelli employee. "This is Mr. Sal Zito. He's been a gem. An absolute jewel. He's taken care of just everything while I've been sick." Then she turned to Sal. "This is Meg, who I told you about. I'm so lucky to be surrounded by such caring people. Caring *and* competent," she added.

Sal Zito acknowledged Meg with a discreet smile that dissolved into a salacious one when he turned back to Shirley. About 65, he was broad and muscular. His face glowed tanning-salon bronze. He was visibly itching to complete his seduction. Shirley wore a fitted gray jacket over a black camisole. Pinned to her lapel was a pink carnation and black satin ribbon with FANELLI'S printed in gold letters. Sal Zito wore an identical corsage.

Meg and Shirley had arranged to go back to Shirley's apartment to talk. Now Meg did not know what to do. She just stood there awkwardly nodding her head. She was certain there was an ill-concealed ironic expression on her face.

Finally, Shirley said, "As soon as I'm 100 percent you can bring Kimmy over. Just a few more days. I hope you don't mind. These stubborn viruses. After the cemetery I'm getting right back into bed. Kimmy is doing as well as can be expected?"

"She refused to eat this morning," said Meg.

"That's normal for now," said Grandma Shirl. "I'll bake her special Gummi Bear cupcakes for her homecoming. She loves those."

Meg simply could not believe the guile of this woman. She let herself flash ahead to her next session with Libby, when she would surely hear, "What! You didn't tell the old bitch off?"

"Shirley, I am not Kimble's guardian. She was a stranger to me until very recently. I'm sorry you're not feeling well, but you and I have to schedule an appointment. What does tomorrow look like for you?"

At this moment Sal signaled to a Fanelli employee posted at the front door. "I'm sorry," he said, hushed, obsequious, now the master of a sober forbearance. "We must begin the procession to the cemetery now." Closing his eyes, he squeezed Shirley Marzola's elbow and steered her ahead of him, as if she were a precious beacon.

∞   ∞   ∞

Ray looked exhausted when Meg appeared to pick up Kimble. He had lost all color. His trademark rhinestone earring—that flash of levity that touted his defiance—merely drew attention to his wan complexion. Meg had heard he was positive and that his T cells were dropping. REACH was a place where the sick shored up the sicker.

Meg touched Ray's arm. His instinctive, joyless smile broke her heart. "Hi, honey. How're you doing?"

"Oh, fine. How's everything here?"

"The usual," said Ray. He looked over Meg's head at some children arguing over an electronic game. The Jolly Players were packing up to go. Still in costume, the wizard put several props into a big black bag. Among the props was the glittering wand. He stuffed it inside the bag with little regard for its sacred function. Next to the stage, Kimble stood watching the wizard. He bustled about, unaware of her presence. No other children were around but Kimble. They had all abandoned her. She stood alone and open-mouthed, gently rocking on her heels as the wizard, who had so recently exalted her, now dismantled himself. Meg was astonished at the insensitivity of the Jolly Players. How could they consider themselves professionals at relating to children when they did not know enough to sustain their illusions? The wizard now stepped out of his satin robe, brushed some lint off the silver lightning rod sewn onto the back, and revealed himself to be an unremarkable-looking young man in black jeans and a tight black T-shirt. Meg was outraged at this stepping out of character. He may as well have unzipped his fly and exposed himself to Kimble. She wanted to say something to Ray, to ask him if he couldn't speak to the Jolly Players about taking their jobs a little more seriously. But by the time Meg turned to speak to Ray he had resolved the dispute over the toy and was tucking in a little boy's shirt. He glanced up at her, then broke out coughing.

Meg came to touch Kimble on the shoulder. "How about if you and I go out for dinner? Just the two of us? You can have french fries."

"He's not a wizard!" declared Kimble. "He's just a stupid *man*!"

Meg was trapped. "He's a wizard *and* a stupid man," she said, tickling Kimble's rib.

"It's not funny. He's not a wizard."

Another character, a wicked queen still in costume, overheard this. She came over.

"He really is a wizard, sweetie," she said. "But when he goes outside he doesn't want people to know he's a wizard. So he dresses in a stupid man's costume."

"You can't talk to me! You're a wicked queen. You're a bitch. Go fish, you bitch!"

"Kimble," said Meg. "I told you last week that language was not allowed. And guess what? It still isn't. This woman is trying to be nice."

"I don't care."

"Well, I care. I'd like you to apologize to her."

This was a refrain from Meg's childhood. She had not been a disobedient child, but she had been a taciturn one, and it seemed Charlotte was forever asking her to apologize to people for not responding to their efforts to please her.

Kimble just stood there, rocking and looking past the mean

queen to the man who used to be the wizard. "I'm not wanting to 'pologize."

Meg was actually frightened that she had started this. To make demands of Kimble on the day of her father's funeral was nothing short of monstrous. "I'll apologize for you this time," she told Kimble. But when she looked into the stranger's eyes, she found that she was fiercely embarrassed. "Sorry," she muttered, like a child herself.

"Oh, listen," dismissed the woman. "Our fault. Evan should've known better." She leaned closer to Meg. "He's new."

"Is Daddy in the van?" Kimble asked Meg, ignoring the queen.

The queen shot Meg an alarmed look. She walked away, but hovered nearby.

"No, honey."

Suddenly Ray was beside her. He bent down. "Kimble, I met your daddy once. Did you know that?"

"No…" said Kimble, suspicious.

"And do you know what he told me?"

"No…"

"He told me he was a very sick man, and he had one wish that was stronger than any other wish. Do you know what it was?"

Kimble shook her head. "*When* did you meet my daddy?"

"Once. Not long ago. He said he wished that if something happened to him, if he left this world to go somewhere else, that you would be happy, that you would let another person who loved you take care of you, and you would have fun with them."

Meg did not know what to say. From the moment she had walked in the door things had gone wrong. Never had she felt such a need to control other people's behavior, to create and monitor their actions. She would not have talked this way to Kimble. She would not have implied her father had gone somewhere else and that he had spoken of her welfare in such a cavalier manner.

"I remember that Daddy died," Kimble now asserted. She seemed to be looking at the queen, who was speaking to Evan, the wizard.

"Are you hungry?" asked Meg. "You must be hungry. Let's get you a whole lot of bad stuff. Hamburgers and french fries and bad stuff."

"Ho Ho's?"

The Jolly Players were filing out the door. The wizard, still in his jeans and T-shirt, had retrieved his wand and came back to wave it in a flurry over Kimble's head.

"You're not a wizard," she told him, and walked over to reclaim her jacket from the coat pegs by the door.

∞   ∞   ∞

When Meg and Kimble got back to the loft that evening there was a message from Charlotte. It was time for their monthly lunch. "Hello, honey. I hope you wrote down Tavern on the Green. I don't know how casual they are these days, but I'd be on the safe side. At least a skirt, please. We can meet at 12:30, all right?"

"Another rhetorical question," Meg said to Kimble. "She's famous for them."

Kimble glanced up in disinterest, then ran to the back of the loft. When she returned, she carried her doll with the roller blades. This time it was dressed in leggings and knee pads. "Roller Queen is not a mean queen. Just the mean queen is mean, but Roller Queen isn't."

"Uh-huh," said Meg. She was opening her mail. The return address on the top letter was from St. Luke's. Inside was a folded piece of napkin. The handwriting was shaky. It said: "This is to make it legel that Shirley Marzola never get costody of my daughter, Kimble Anita Toffler. Very Sincerely, Barry Joseph Toffler."

"Can I have roller blades?"

"Sometime."

"When?"

Meg simply wanted to banish Kimble. Like the Jolly Player's wizard, she wanted to wave her wand and make Kimble go away. She could not answer questions about time ("When?"). She could not answer questions about money ("Can I have...?"). She wanted nothing more than the luxury to think, to plan, in peace. This constancy was what would undermine her, would make her say, *No, I can't do this.* In one imperceptible stroke she had gone from someone driving every aspect of her own life to an empty vessel, one of her own unfinished and unadorned pots, there to fill up a child's needs, to be filled and drained at whim by a child who had not yet developed enough long-term memory to retain the fact of her own father's death. At once Meg was filled with pity and trepidation. It seemed only fair that children and adults should negotiate a compromise in which they took turns occupying the same space. But no, the tyranny of children was their categorical *thereness.*

"When can I have roller blades?"

"Children as young as you don't have roller blades," said Meg. Was this true? It seemed so.

"Why not?"

"I have to make a call now, Kimmy. Why don't you turn on the TV? Is Mr. Rogers on?"

"No! It's night. Just stupid violence."

Meg smiled. Kimble had gotten this from her.

"Turn on the TV anyway. I'll be right there, I promise."

Kimble did as she was told. Meg grabbed the phone. This was not to be premeditated. She just wanted to get it behind her.

"Hi."

"Hello, dear. You got my message? 12:30 tomorrow, then? Or we could make it 1 o'clock. Either is convenient for me."

"Well, actually, I don't think I can make it."

"All right," said Charlotte coolly. "We'll reschedule. But it must be soon. I'm leaving in just two weeks, you know."

"Oh, jeez, I forgot. How's it coming? Are you ready?"

"Meg, why can't you make it tomorrow? You know this is a standing date. Why didn't you call me before this?"

"I still have that client's kid."

Charlotte did not immediately respond. When Meg was a girl, Charlotte would automatically say, "A kid is a billy goat."

"All right, I can see this is serious now. What's going on?"

"I have a lot to think about. There are some complicated issues here."

"Forget issues. What in the world is going on down there?"

Charlotte called Duane Street "down there" because it was south of Park Avenue, but Meg knew the expression handily doubled as an allusion to the pit of hell.

"I'm not going to talk to you if you're going to get like this."

"I want to know what you're doing with that child. This is all very mysterious. For heaven's sake, you can't expect me not to wonder. One could argue you are orchestrating this whole buildup just for suspense, Meg."

"Uh-huh," said Meg. "One could." She had neither the wherewithal to respond nor to hang up. She was in a state she associated only with Charlotte, a state of physical suspension in which the animate stirrings within her body—her breathing, even the natural churning of digestive fluids—all seemed to stop and wait. Her very insides were held in a chaste and excruciating pose.

"Meg, please do me the courtesy of responding. I have the right to know what's happening down there."

Ah, the *right*, thought Meg.

"Mom, I'm just really tired right now. I've had a long day. You can come down here tomorrow, if you want. It is just too hard for me to get up there this time."

"All right, fine. I will come down there. 12:30. Do you think I should put the Galapagos on hold?"

"No. Why?"

"I don't know, Meg. I just thought you might need me."

"Oh," said Meg, who for so long had needed only not to need Charlotte. "I'm sorry. Of course you should go to the Galapagos. This is not a tragedy; there is no tragedy occurring here."

"Well, all right, I just know how you are about tragedy."

"What's that supposed to mean?" Meg demanded.

"Oh, Meg, please. Don't be so sensitive."

"What did you mean?"

"Well, it's not the worst thing in the world, really. You just seem to be somewhat drawn to tragedy, don't you agree?"

"That was a fairly unforgivable thing to say." A certain energy made these words swell in Meg's mouth; she brought them forth as if in song.

∞　　∞　　∞

Meg had long since stopped compromising her style of

dress to appease Charlotte. On more than one occasion she had shown up for their monthly luncheons in leggings, an oversize sweater, an Indonesian scarf whose fringes her mother had called scraggly, and a black leather jacket. Yet after this last phone conversation with Charlotte, Meg and Kimble had rushed up to a children's specialty shop on Madison Avenue. There Meg had purchased a hand-knit Irish wool cardigan, an appliquéd skirt, and a navy-and-green tartan jumper imported from Edinburgh. To go with the jumper she had chosen a powder-blue cotton shirt with Peter Pan collar and piped sleeves. Of course, the idea of Kimble wearing any of these outfits to accompany Meg along her routine errands in TriBeCa was ridiculous. Meg imagined the two of them at her usual Saturday diner—Kimble, sweet shepherdess to hookers, johns, and runaways.

Meg had gone directly from *Wee Little People* to see Libby, and they had discussed the purchase of these little-girl outfits. Libby had entered into this discussion with great relish. Here was Meg presenting her mother with sugar and spice, a perfect little angel in the form of a junkie's daughter. "What a wonderful put-down," complimented Libby. But Meg did not see her purchases as a wily stroke against Charlotte. The outfits were some kind of bait, and the sad thing about it was that Meg was not even sure what they were supposed to reel in.

∞   ∞   ∞

At 12:30 the next day, Charlotte rang the bell. She had not been to the loft in two years and in fact had seen it only once. The matter of the loft was rarely discussed; Charlotte's complete disapproval was implicit. She knew the conditions of its legality were very complex, and she could not understand why

Meg would voluntarily involve herself with such complications. The appearance and location of the loft were beneath
mention, so when Meg came to open the huge tin-covered
door to Duane Street, and then when she hoisted her mother
up in the manual elevator (the walls decorated by the downstairs painter, Chris, with somber prints depicting medieval
Crusades), Charlotte offered only a terse greeting and a nervous smile. Moments later, when Kimble ran to meet the elevator outside the third-floor loft, when she stood before
Charlotte in her tartan jumper, her wispy hair held back with
two navy barrettes, Charlotte looked neither at Kimble nor at
Meg but at the de Chirico poster next to Meg's door and asked,
"You let this child alone in this place for 30 seconds?"

As if in direct response, Kimble nodded her head and
remarked, "I'm Kimble Toffler. My daddy just died."

"Let's all go in," said Meg. She stepped forward, took
Kimble by the hand, and led her through the long storage hall
where unglazed pots and molds were stored on metal shelves.

Once inside, Meg made her way to the slab stone countertop in the kitchen, leaned against it, crossed her arms, and
waited. Before too many seconds had passed, she asked,
"Would you like something? Herbal tea? I've got Cinnamon
Rose, Mellow Mint, and, I think, English Breakfast. Are you
hungry? I could make tuna melts."

"Yeah! Tuna melts!" said Kimble.

Charlotte looked about the loft. Her expression was withheld, severe. Meg did not know if her mother was angry
because she had not prepared lunch or because Meg had
apparently decided to take up a permanent life in this loft.

"You probably don't want a tuna melt, Mom. I have fresh
fruit. Would you like a salad?"

"I'll eat with Kimble," said Charlotte. The remark may as

well have been the starting gun that began the competition.

Meg told her mother to take Kimble over to the couch while she prepared lunch. As she laid out plates with pickles and pota-to chips, she listened to Charlotte and Kimble. Meg was sur-prised at how Charlotte was able to project her voice into a reg-ister that wafted far above her usual woebegone timbre. When the tuna melts were ready, Meg carried two plates out to the pol-ished liberty-ship door that served as her coffee table. Kimble wanted to carry the third plate and made an ordeal of climbing on the high stool to get it, then carried it back with exaggerated care. Meg and her mother watched. As if stunned, they watched in silence. They did not look at each other.

During lunch, Meg listened as Charlotte asked Kimble several questions. Adults were subjected to this same style of inquiry. Charlotte's objective was always the same: to deter-mine if she were speaking to a person of quality. Many times Meg had squirmed in embarrassment as her mother had clumsily attempted to measure the cultivation and intelli-gence of new acquaintances. This afternoon, though, she was genuinely curious to see if Kimble would intuit the nature of Charlotte's delving.

"That's an awfully pretty outfit you're wearing, Kimble. Can you name all the colors in it?"

"Green and navy-blue, and navy-blue and green," sang Kimble.

Great, thought Meg. Brilliant, actually, since green domi-nated the skirt of her jumper, navy the straps.

"I think you're still too young for school, is that right?" asked Charlotte.

"Yes. But I'm almost old enough for kindergarten."

"And what about day care? Do you go to day care?"

Kimble turned toward Meg.

"Day care is like Ray's playroom," Meg explained.

"Yes," said Kimble. "At REACH. Jackie has AIDS. So does Tito and Chantelle and Pauly. And my daddy did, but he died. I told you he died. But Kevin doesn't have it, and neither do I have it."

Charlotte busied herself cutting the crusts off her tuna melt. She recrossed her legs. She brushed some crumbs off her Armani skirt. "Do you have a napkin, Meg?" she asked.

"Oh, sure. Sorry. I laid them out." Meg went back to get the cloth napkins she had fit inside some alabaster rings that Sarina had picked up at a flea market years before. When she came back, Kimble was showing Charlotte a plastic ruby ring that the Jolly Players had given her to mark her stature as Princess.

Charlotte admired the ring. Then she said, "I bet you'd love a nap after lunch."

"I don't take naps. Meg does sometimes."

Meg felt herself blush. A child, she should have realized, is an untrustworthy guardian of secret habits. "Why don't you finish your potato chips and go back on the futon and try to take a little nap? Then you can stay up later tonight."

Kimble's eyes began to well up with tears. Meg had a strong urge to hold her, to fold her into her arms and smooth back her incredibly soft hair, but she was far too self-conscious. "Want me to tuck you in?"

"Yes. And then maybe I'll sleep, and maybe I won't. And maybe Roller Queen will sleep, and maybe she won't."

When Meg came back, Charlotte was cleaning off the slab stone countertop with a dirty kitchen sponge. She did not look up. "She sleeps on a futon?"

"For now."

"And later?" Charlotte pulled a stool up to the countertop

and sat down. She straightened up and massaged the small of her back. "Meg, I can understand you wanting to have a child. This does not surprise me. I am not surprised. I have long known this was not a resolved issue, but this is gravely serious. Have you any idea that this is serious business, that this is another human being?"

Meg looked at her mother's face, at the new, glossy, Venetian-red lipstick that as recently as two months ago she had bought for Meg as well as herself, assuring Meg that with their identical colorings it would be the perfect shade for her. What did Charlotte mean by "another human being"?

"You don't even know what's happening." Meg sat down on the stool across from her mother.

"I know what's happening. You want to rescue a child. This is heroic, yes, but it is problematic too."

"I don't want to be a hero!" claimed Meg. There were volumes more to say ("The simple, crisp truth," as Libby would have it), but the words would not dislodge themselves.

"That wasn't right of me," said Charlotte. "I'm sorry. I believe in maternal needs. You know I do. I see in you very deep maternal needs, Meg. All this independence you've forged for yourself, you think you've forged for yourself—it has not supplanted your basic maternal needs."

"I'm not really ready to talk about this," said Meg weakly.

"There are many alternatives, Meg. This is not Bangladesh or Biafra, for heaven's sake. We take care of our children."

"Jesus, Mom! Wake up! We *don't* take care of our children."

"Well," soothed Charlotte, "right now perhaps you don't want to think we do, but—"

"We don't. We take care of little newborns, and some very few people—the saints out there—take in sick or disabled orphans. The rest rot."

"All right, let's just get off your high horse now. As usual, you're taking things to their furthest extreme. You and I both know that little white girls...and don't jump down my throat, Meg. I didn't make the world."

"She's four-and-a-half years old. Each month of age decreases her desirability. And *both* her parents died of AIDS. She's fine, but plenty of people are still superstitious. So..."

"This is very interesting to me, Meg. It's very interesting that you're exaggerating her plight. I'm interested to see how you mold the facts to serve your needs. Your father, by the way, was very good at that. That's why he was such a good businessman."

"I haven't quite decided what to do yet. Kimmy has this grandmother, the mother's mother, and she has custody now. I'll have to deal with her. She doesn't want Kimble, but for some reason she's saying she does. There's a lot I need to know, research I have to do."

Charlotte was not paying attention. She ran her fingers over the rim of Meg's russet-colored pot. "Perhaps you think you can resolve some of our conflicts through a relationship with this little girl, but—"

"Bullshit!"

"Swearing!" came Kimble's jubilant voice from behind the partition.

"*Subconsciously*, I mean," whispered Charlotte.

Meg stood up. As she did, she felt the effort of every engaged muscle in her legs. She had the unreasonable thought that her muscles were far older than those of her mother. "Go to the Galapagos, Mom. Enjoy yourself. We'll talk when you get back."

"Anything might happen while I'm gone!" burst out Charlotte. Her eyes were wild.

"Yes, anything might," agreed Meg. Her purposeful tone gleaned the few bits of mastery left to her inside the moment.

6

As Charlotte Krantz headed for the Galapagos on a newly renovated cruise liner, Meg drove to southern Jersey to sell her pots at the Somerset Crafts Fair. Kimble was belted in beside her, chattering about the Kimble pot that Meg had promised her when they returned. "Will it have my whole face or just part of my face? Will it be pretty or ugly?"

Meg answered without concentrating. She had discovered that if she met Kimble's prattle with equally silly answers, Kimble would rock gently back and forth as if they were engaged in a musical collaboration. "Of course it will be pretty. Ravishing, in fact," she said. Her mind was neither on Kimble nor the Kimble pot. It was on Cami Porter.

Meg had met Cami her first year at Somerset. Brassy and garrulous, Cami was artistic in a way that made Meg nervous. She crafted origami and papier-mâché jewelry. Although the shapes of her origami earrings were whimsical, she could not let well enough alone. She sprayed the earrings with Glitter Glow. The papier-mâché bracelets were dotted with raindrops and teardrops, star bursts and cat's eyes. This jewelry sold at a phenomenal rate.

The first year at Somerset, Meg had moved two pots in three days. She had spent the entire fair reading *The White Goddess*. The success of Cami Porter had disgusted all of the exhibitors that year. Several times Somerset's organizers had come around to report Cami's sales figures. This was meant to encourage. It didn't; everyone had seen Cami's work. The origami earrings were really talismans, Meg had told her neighbor; they threw a magnetic field over people's wallets.

That first year Meg had exhausted herself packing and unpacking several times over. She had decided to stay the night at her motel before driving back to Manhattan. It was then that Cami, exhilarated by her success, introduced herself and asked if she could buy Meg a drink.

From the start, their affair had been gloriously devoid of expectation. It had begun two weeks later, when Cami drove from Delaware to New York to consign her earrings to some gift shops. In bed with Cami, Meg had become other people. Encouraged by Cami's laughter and by the quick arching of her back, she had transformed herself into a turn-of-the-century Shaker schoolmarm, a virgin whose thwarted sex drive had left her afflicted with a constant quivering. She had become Baroness Dripping In It, who spent her untold fortune importing nymphs from Pacific islands. She had even become Ben Benson, a dutiful husband who one night embraced his unlived life in the men's room of the Larchmont train station. To Meg's amazement, she had introduced all these characters during a single week in New York and had embellished on them at the Somerset Crafts Fairs that followed.

The duration of this affair was a wonder to them both. Meg clung to the unworthy thought that Cami was a bit in awe of her. Cami had it fixed in her mind that Meg's pots were profoundly literary, that they served up mythological messages that changed people's lives. Only once did Meg argue that people used her pottery as a receptacle for their laundry tickets and spare keys. She let Cami believe as she did. Cami's admiration often led to a flurry of touches, then to the lovemaking that pulled Meg into the sorrow beneath Cami's incessant smile. And then later more appreciation, another flurry of touches, would conjure Baroness Dripping In It, or the Shaker schoolmarm whose legs Cami parted with excruciating patience, or Ben Benson, whose phantom penis between Meg's legs swelled as she described his predawn life in the Larchmont station men's room.

This autumn, her sixth at Somerset, Meg walked up to Cami's booth, holding Kimble Toffler by the hand. Of course she had written to Cami, had told her she was in a weird place with this kid who had been summoned into her life. (Cami thought people were summoned into one another's lives. Meg believed all occurrence was random. She believed that beyond the injustices ushered in by birthright, all was random.)

"Here she is. Her Royal Highness, Kimble Anita Toffler. Kimble, this is my friend Cami Porter."

"Cami *what* Porter?" Kimble wanted to know.

Meg looked up at Cami, who gazed back at her with open lust. The suggestion of motherhood had done it.

"Well, actually, I don't know. Cami what Porter?" she asked Cami. They could barely look at each other. What was more erotic than having to assume a platonic friendship in front of a little girl who favored Victorian prints?

"Cami Toosdaneldanewspickle Porter."

Kimble clamped two rosy-knuckled fists over her mouth. Her cheeks puffed up, and her shoulders shook with laughter. "It is *not*!"

"It truly is," said Cami. My mother's mother was Toosdanelda and my father's mother was Newspickle. So I honor both my grandmothers."

"Anita was my mother's name," said Kimble.

"Would you like a pair of earrings?" asked Cami. "What's your favorite bird?"

"Bluebird. 'Cause they're on my underpants. They're underpants birds."

"Well, I don't have bluebirds, so how about a pair of ruby-throated hummingbirds wearing top hats?"

"Yeah!"

Cami removed Kimble's earrings and fit in the humming-birds. The little gold posts were one of the first things Meg had noticed when she met Kimble. She knew she was being a snob, but she had never liked pierced ears on small children; the tiny earrings always struck her as symbols of an arranged marriage with God. Yet she had never dared to remove Kimble's earrings.

The weather that first day put people into a buying mood. The breeze never stilled. Clouds raced through the sky, blocking and revealing the sun at dramatic will. Following a streak of heavy, airless weather, this breeze invigorated, reminded people of the blood flowing in their veins. Spurred by the sensual weather, people got the notion to buy themselves into deeper rapture. Color people ran to Cami. Form people ran to Meg. Kimble ran between them. At Cami's she painstakingly wrapped pairs of earrings with fuchsia tissue, put the tissue inside a marble-patterned bag, and closed the bag with a gold seal that said CAMI PORTER, LTD. At Meg's she sprinkled hand-fuls of excelsior over the pots that Meg had rolled in bubble wrap and packed into their boxes. In exchange for Kimble's labor, Meg and Cami promised they would buy her a linen pinafore on display at the Pennsylvania Dutch booth. The pinafore had embroidered sheep and corncobs circling its hem.

Kimble was in the highest spirits. Twice Meg had watched her helping Cami and thought that no one would ever suspect what this child had been through.

Back at Meg's around 4 o'clock, Kimble handed over a piece of folded paper sealed with Cami's gold sticker. Meg was discussing a new fertility drug with a woman and her husband. The couple looked at Kimble solemnly, then told Meg she did beautiful work and moved on.

"Oh, so she's hired you as a messenger too? I don't know," mused Meg as she opened the paper. "That might be taking unfair advantage."

"It's not," said Kimble, wounded. "What does it say?"

The message was that Cami had a local friend who was taking two of her kids to see their sister perform in *The Mikado* at Somerset High that night. The friend had offered to take Kimble along.

"What does it say?"

"Here, honey. Take this back to Cami. On the back of the paper Meg had written: "Ever the schemer—B.D.I.I."

Kimble strained to read the last letters. "B…D. What's the next one, Meg?"

"I," said Meg. "Just a bunch of silly letters, honey. I'm just being silly."

∞   ∞   ∞

The decor of the motel rooms they had stayed in over the years had always served to reunite them. It interested Meg that Cami's origami and papier-mâché jewelry did not reflect her serious taste; they were merely barter in a tacky world. It had become ritual to critique the motel room as soon as they entered it. This evening Cami noticed the bedside lamp first. "Did I ever tell you," she asked, "how I've longed to own a ceramic log entwined with ivy?"

"No!" exclaimed Meg. "I didn't know this about you. But, of course, I've been too obsessed with trying to get my hands on an original painting of the Statue of Liberty framed by cameos of our founding fathers."

"Yes," said Cami, "I can see how my own longing would seem petty to a great patriot like you."

"Your longings? Petty?" responded Meg on cue. And so the evening began. But only the beginning resembled the evenings Meg had grown to expect with Cami. Cami was wonderfully herself, but Meg had become, since last year, someone else. She lingered on the surface and had neither the mettle nor the desire to go deeper. She could feel Cami bridle herself, reluctant to betray unwelcome passion, but Meg could not let loose. She kept flashing on *The Mikado*, way above Kimble's head—a play that would cause her mind to wander and notice she was in the company of strangers in a place she had never been before. Suddenly Meg lurched up and switched on the unspeakable bedside lamp. "You're sure you gave your friend this number?"

"Twice," said Cami, blinking.

"It was a mistake," said Meg. "I should have gone too."

Cami sat up. She rested her head on the backboard—plastic-covered velveteen. Meg heard a hiss when Cami's head made contact, but she said nothing. Cami lit a cigarette.

"Can I have one?"

"You're kidding."

"No." Meg put out two fingers and Cami slipped a Merit between them. "What am I going to do?" she asked.

"Stop masticating. You want to adopt her, do it. You don't, don't."

"Whoa. You're pissed, aren't you?"

"Baroness Dripping In It doesn't ruminate. She acts." Cami was thoughtful for a moment. "She buys floozies and tarts from the four corners of the world. Here she has one imported from the heart of exotic downtown Somerset. A rare find. A once-in-a-lifetime opportunity."

"I'm not the Baroness," countered Meg. "I'm the Shaker schoolmarm."

Cami laughed. "In spades."

Meg drew on the Merit. It had been seven years since she had smoked a cigarette. Although she coughed, she quickly recovered and took another drag. When she had quit, it hadn't been quite for the conventional reasons. The first cigarette of the day had always kicked up a cold dread, an enormously physical dread, a bodily response to mortal danger. Maybe adrenaline was involved, but the effect of first lighting up was a prevision of death. Meg felt this same moribund sensation now. She snuffed out the cigarette. "I know I'm ruminating," she conceded, "but this is really tough stuff, Cami."

"So what's next?"

Cami was what Charlotte called a "doer."

"I don't know. You know I'm illegal here. This whole thing is incredible; I'm actually kidnapping her. REACH thinks the grandmother has her. The social worker at St. Luke's thinks so too. Shirley—that's the grandmother—signed some temporary-custody papers, and she's going to be accountable soon. I have to confront this part of the mess no matter what I decide."

"So what's with the grandmother?" Cami looked weary yet intensely interested.

"I don't know. There's some history there. There has to be— she drove the kid's mother to a convent."

"Don't you think you should talk to her?"

"Jesus, I don't want to. But I have to. Soon."

"Yes," said Cami, putting out her cigarette. She pushed some hair away from Meg's face. "You do." Her voice was hushed, regardful.

"Cami, I don't know what to do." Meg's voice broke. "I know I'm being indecisive, the old 'pathologically indecisive woman' thing, but this is so big. Yes, I know, millions of women do it…they're half my age, and they don't think twice about it. Why's it so big for me?"

Cami didn't answer for a moment. Meg was afraid she was going to say, "Only you can answer that."

Instead Cami said, "It's easier for two." Her words were barely audible. Her words were measured. "It's undeniably half as hard if there are two parents. Two incomes."

It was then that Meg put her finger on why the room was such an affront: its uncanny stillness. There was not one suggestion of movement, not one dynamic convergence of shapes. And no air. There were two sets of drapes, inner and outer, both so thick a breeze would not stir them. The brown and olive tones of the carpet reflected no light. The ceiling was low, and its cheerful, selfsame plaster swirls were an insult to the spirit. The only sound in the stout, rectangular room was the rattling of its baseboard heaters.

"Maybe you don't need to hear this, but I think two parents are better," repeated Cami. "It's just a whole hell of a lot easier."

Meg closed her eyes. Once, three-and-a-half years ago, at a time when her business foundered and Cami's throve, she had driven to Delaware for a long weekend. Along the drive she had pictured a future with Cami. Presented in her mind was a life both passionate and orderly, and Meg thought it might be sustained. But during the weekend she had seen the passion was pure sensation, and the order was tedium. As Sunday night drew near, the yapping of Cami's Pekingese swelled to become the sound of enemy gunfire. Meg wanted nothing more than to be in her van heading up I-95, Keith Jarrett coming from her speakers.

Although Meg now tightly squeezed Cami's hand and wriggled beneath the sheets, she kept her eyes closed to mourn the death of the Shaker schoolmarm, Baroness Dripping In It, and the pitiable Ben Benson. It was then that she finally let loose. She stretched and improvised on what little love there was, as if that love were a mound of intractable clay rising on the wheel, clay that would finally buckle under Meg's overwrought touch.

∞   ∞   ∞

In the parking lot of the fairgrounds late the next day, Kimble sat on a rock and examined the hem of her new pinafore. Meg was in and out of the van, repacking stock. She had called Kimble twice, but Kimble had ignored her. Now Meg approached the rock. "Come on, Kimmy," she said.

"I'm coming," answered Kimble without looking up. Meg could see the hem had become her world. She could not bear to take her eyes from it, and Meg suddenly remembered the absolute and private immersions of her own childhood. Kimble held up the hem in one hand and fingered it with the other. In turn, she petted each tiny, embroidered sheep. She poked at the corncobs, trying to smooth their miniature husks between her own tiny fingernails. She crouched farther down; her lips moved in obeisance.

"Come on, honey, we're going back, now."

Slowly Kimble raised her head. For an instant, Meg thought

she had seen some bucolic countryside—had seen beyond the radius they had traveled. Kimble's complexion was drained of color, her green eyes unnaturally bright. "What about Toosda Nelda? What about Toosda Nelda Newspickle?"

"She doesn't live in New York."

"Why not?"

"I don't know. I guess she doesn't like it."

"I want her to come with us."

Not for the first time, Meg's feelings were hurt. She had to get over this, she told herself; she had to talk to Libby about this.

"Well, I'm sure she'd like to, but she can't right now. Why don't you just get into the van?"

"Toosda Nelda won't come 'cause you don't want her to."

"Kimble, are you coming or not? Because I can just leave you here, if that's what you want."

Kimble went back to talking to her hem. Meg felt her ears flame. By any standard she was a monster. To speak to a parentless child like this! Libby would not do; Libby was the perfect therapist for people whose years of prior therapy had already set them on course. Meg did not know who she could go to with this.

"Baby, I didn't mean that, I would never leave you behind. Never in a million years. Are you tired? Do you want me to carry you?"

Kimble just sat there, and Meg scooped her up, grateful for the second chance. They drove together for 50 miles, Kimble belted in and padded up with pillows. She wheezed in her sleep, and Meg kept reaching out to pet her left hand, cupped into a fist around her blossom of gathered hem. Finally, Meg pulled into a Howard Johnson's.

Inside the dining room a waitress came with Kimble's order.

The hot dog looked rubbery, and the beans were covered in a thin, orange-colored sauce. Kimble ignored the plate being put down in front of her. She pointed to a squirrel that scaled a sapling outside the window. Then, as she turned toward the waitress, her neck suddenly grew so taut that shallows appeared on either side of her windpipe. First, all color drained from her face. Then an urgent, scolding red appeared—soared from her neck to the crown of her head. No breaths; only sucking noises from her mouth. Her chest moved not up and down but sideways, it seemed: violent and arrhythmic. Meg was up in a flash running for the pay phone in the lobby.

"Let me," said the waitress, and hastily put the plate down in the middle of the table. She overtook Meg, motioning her back like a traffic cop.

"9-1-1!" yelled Meg. "My God, 9-1-1!"

Back at the booth, Meg lifted Kimble out of her booster seat, laid her facedown on the booth seat, then dug the heels of her hands into Kimble's back, below her rib cage. She had no idea what she was doing, beyond forcing air into Kimble's lungs, nor why she was doing it. Kimble's feet pushed back against Meg's thighs.

"They're on their way," said the waitress, a woman in her fifties with a dyed black bowl cut. "What should I tell them? What is this?"

"I don't know," said Meg, ashamed of her ignorance, terrified at its possible consequences. She turned Kimble over. Kimble was still wild in her attempts to capture air. The delicate contour of her features, the blurry edges that marked her looks as ethereal, were now bold lines; Meg saw her features focus into an adult's as her fear deepened.

"Honey, it's asthma! My nephew has it," declared the waitress, jubilant. "You don't have an atomizer?"

Meg just shook her head in wonder, convinced for a moment that Kimble really did have an atomizer, that she had come with one like Roller Queen came with knee pads, and that for all this time Meg had neglected to notice it.

Kimble gasped and wheezed thickly, and she knocked away Meg's comforting hand. The ambulance siren attained its highest pitch right outside the window where Meg stood.

∞   ∞   ∞

As Kimble was being seen by an emergency-room intern, Meg had forms to deal with, and these forms turned out to be an arsenal of menacing questions. In the end, Meg had to confess to the admissions clerk that she could not provide the answers the forms were after. She told the woman behind the desk that Kimble had no parents. She told her that Kimble's grandmother was the little girl's temporary guardian and she was sorry that Mrs. Marzola was not here to sign the papers. As it happened, Meg said, she was a friend of Shirley's who had taken Kimble to the Somerset Crafts Fair for the weekend and was delivering her home when this horrible thing had happened. The woman looked at her askance, particularly when Meg's pencil hovered over the section of the form marked "Patient's Medical History." It was now that Meg regretted she had never read Barry and Kimble's client intake report. But neither had Tina told her that Kimble had asthma. Maybe, then, this was her first attack.

"How much will this be?" Meg asked, eager to seem financially responsible. She opened her wallet to survey her credit cards.

"It depends on what's required," said the woman blandly. "Does the guardian have insurance?"

"No, I'll pay."

At this, the woman presented another form, which she asked Meg to sign. It assured that if an insurance claim for emergency service was declined, Meg would be responsible for the bill. Meg signed it without hesitation.

At 2 o'clock in the morning Meg emerged from the hospital pharmacy with a bronchodilator and something called cromolyn sodium that the doctor told her would reduce the inflammation that had made this attack so frightening. While Kimble was hooked up to an IV, the doctor had explained that they were now taking a two-pronged approach to asthma management: reducing inflammation at the same time as they tried to reverse bronchial constriction. Kimble would probably grow out of her attacks before adolescence, he had said. "In the meantime," he warned, "you'll have to be alert to the sound of her breathing. The object," he said, gesturing to Kimble behind the open curtain, "is to catch it before it gets to this point."

Meg had thanked him, and she and Kimble had spent the rest of the night at the hospital, asleep or resting. Still shaken, Meg was reluctant to leave this small, suburban hospital—this refuge where everyone who entered was expected to be helpless. When two nurses told Meg they really should prepare the space for the morning, Meg got up, worked on Kimble's Dalmatian sneakers, and began to lead her to the lobby. Breathing clearly now, Kimble lifted her arms to be picked up, a thing she had never done before. Meg carried her to the van. Rather than belt her in, she allowed Kimble to stretch across the front seat. As they entered the Holland Tunnel and passed to the New York side, Kimble burrowed her head farther into Meg's lap. Meg said nothing about the danger, about what could happen if they stopped short. She just let Kimble lie there, silently fingering a button on Meg's sweater, trying to mate it with one of the embroidered sheep along the stiff hem of her new pinafore.

At home that weekend, Kimble posed for her Kimble pot, a clay piece that ended up envisioning some future Kimble, a wide-cheeked, jocular face framed by upswept curls. Meg coiled the curls into a lid and fashioned a top knot for a handle. The Kimble pot would be a cookie jar, said Meg, and they would keep it stocked with Ho Ho's and Twinkies. But Meg knew that each time she looked at the Kimble pot she would see a small monument to a merciless era, a time in which addled strangers rushed toward children whose existence had never before mattered to them.

7

"You spend an awful lot of time harping on this topic," said Libby.

It was Tuesday afternoon, and Meg was sitting in Libby's blue leather recliner, to the right of an Alfred Sisley reproduction that was hung too low. "That's what I love about you, Libby. How you never veer from orthodox Freudian technique."

Libby smiled. The topic was privilege. In her therapy Meg had continually returned to the guilt she felt in having led such a privileged childhood.

"Well, harping has its uses," said Libby. Her reversals were part of her diversified approach.

"I just can never reconcile the lives they led with the life I lead."

"Why should you have to?"

Meg said nothing.

"And why should you be expected to lead their lives?"

"I'm not, but plenty of people do, you know." Meg could not believe how petulant she sounded. "A lot of the children of my parents' friends turned out to be their parents all over again."

"Am I supposed to congratulate you? I could, I suppose. I could be your cheerleader. But I would automatically expect far more of you than turning into your mother. How is she, by the way?"

"Who knows? She's with Ida Tree and Juliet what's-her-name, Ida's daughter. Juliet's getting divorced, so they took her to the Galapagos. You know, the more tawdry the divorce, the more exotic the cure. It's an unwritten decree."

Most sessions would find Libby inching toward the edge of her seat, eager to hear the details of the decadent holiday. This morning Libby remained silent. She looked at Meg and sighed.

"She wanted me to come with them!" continued Meg, outraged. "Can you imagine? To them, all that amazing wildlife exists for the sole purpose of distracting Juliet what's her-name from her messy divorce. They have no idea how vulgar they are. My mother thinks she's refined."

"I bet you'd love to go to the Galapagos," mused Libby.

"You think I should have gone with them."

"Not at all," Libby came back. She sounded sincere. Meg was always relieved to have her misgivings countered. She desperately needed Libby's encouragement not to give in to her mother. Again, Meg was the customer and Libby the vendor. Over and over Meg had to purchase a free conscience. She was 37 years old, and she was in school to earn a child's clear conscience.

"Why don't you go to the Galapagos alone?" suggested Libby. "You're a free agent."

This was typical. It would not be enough to help Meg feel all right about having refused the trip. Libby would have her turn around and fly to Ecuador at the very hour her mother returned.

"So the idea here is that if you suggest something so extreme, so *sadistic*, I'll feel OK about acting with normal independence."

Libby did not smile. "Aren't you a little old to be playing the precocious child?"

Meg looked over Libby's head, at an Ansel Adams poster of giant redwoods, this one hung too high. "Anyway," she said, "I'm not a free agent anymore. I have Kimble now."

Libby examined her nail polish and waited.

"I'm trying to remember what I thought it was going to be like when I grew up," offered Meg.

"Explain."

"Not just me but all privileged kids in the '60s. We were wafting on the efforts of an underclass, and we didn't think twice about it. It was amazing. My mother still doesn't think twice about it. My friends and I would lie in chaises around the pool at that obscene country club in Westchester, and we would Coppertone ourselves to death and talk clothes allowances and then go to the clubhouse and charge huge amounts of food to our parents' accounts. Steak tartare at 2 o'clock in the afternoon, for Christ's sake! I'm telling you, it never occurred to us that full-grown adults were making a living, were living their lives waiting on us. We never looked at them, we never thought about them, we lived in total oblivion."

"So now you have to repent for the rest of your life," offered Libby flatly.

"What did I think my life would be about? I think I thought it would just continue. Us and them, forever and ever."

"What did you do when your friends turned to the topic of boys?" Libby broke in. She was genuinely interested.

"Sidestepped. I got away with it too. I capitalized on this arty, independent image. It amused them that I was not interested in boys. It made me sort of a team mascot. Like a neutered goat."

Libby nodded but did not smile. "So you were independent then?"

"Very. Independence in the context of complete financial security is my forte."

"And what are you now?"

Meg surveyed the big, airy room where Libby spent so much time. It was less opulent than any room in her mother's apartment yet far more homey than any area in Meg's loft. "I don't know."

"What would it take for you to be independent, Meg?"

"If I earned a fortune, I guess."

"Stop it. We don't have all afternoon." Libby reached behind her. When she turned around she had a cigarette.

"What happened to the patch? Didn't it work?"

"Never mind about that."

"Real money would make this adoption decision a lot easier."

Libby nodded. "I understand that. So why don't you ask her? I don't believe it would make you more dependent. I believe it would enable you to do something that would make you feel like a more complete person."

Meg was unable to reply. It was one of those moments in Libby's office when there was too much to ward off. She had spent many years treasuring her solitude and the freedom of her love life. Before Kimble, the suggestion that her childlessness would make her feel incomplete would have been ludicrous. After all, it was the most common notion patriarchy had to offer. But at home this past weekend with Kimble, fashioning her features onto the wet clay she had just thrown, making her tenderness palpable, there had come a physical drive to protect that had overwhelmed Meg. It was a force that compelled this child not within her but above her. *Your life will drive mine* was the unspoken message. The words had seemed to emerge from some moldering past, and they scared Meg more than she could possibly convey to Libby.

"I won't feel more complete," she finally managed. "I don't know what I'll feel."

"You're afraid she'll consume you," said Libby. "You're afraid she'll consume you in the way you have consumed your mother."

How many times in this office had her most basic forebodings been made so unequivocal? Meg said nothing.

"This is understandable, Meg. You have not yet done all that is necessary for your mother to stop being consumed by you. So it is easy for you to imagine being permanently consumed by Kimble."

"What should I do, Libby?" Meg felt her face heat up. "I live in another world—socially, politically, sexually. I make my own living. I fend her off at every pass. What should I seriously do to make myself independent? Should I wave good-bye to her in the airport while she's arriving from the Galapagos and I'm going there?"

Libby released a luxurious stream of smoke through her nose and snuffed out the cigarette. "No," she answered. "You should ask her for money to help you raise the child of a heroin addict."

Although this had the tone of any of Libby's efforts to provoke, although she framed it in a glib, even singsong voice, Meg immediately saw its intelligence. Libby knew exactly what she was talking about. "I can't do that," she said.

"You imagine that you have grown beyond an us-and-them mentality, that you are more socially liberated. But this is not true. You have the opportunity to give Kimble a life, and you are afraid to do it because your mother thinks she's one of them. How does that make you better than your mother?"

"I'm not better than my mother."

"You insist that you live in a different world than she does. I think you *observe* a different world than she does. That's very nice, but it's not living."

Again Meg looked around Libby's consultation room. There was a fireplace, a big oak desk, two lush Boston ferns flanking a wall of leaded windows, framed posters and water-colors, a Turkish rug over an old parquet floor. What did Libby know of crack dens and living past the margins? But then, for all of Libby's unorthodox methods, Meg really knew little about her life.

"Meg...Describe to me the kind of mother you would like to be."

"Casual, Libby. I'd like to be a casual mother. I don't want to interpret the world for Kimble. I don't want to ply her with lessons and make sure she knows they are meant to enrich her life. I don't want to probe her inner world and imagine there are kernels of genius there. I don't want to describe her in lofty terms to my friends. I want her life to be separate from mine, and I don't think I can do it."

Libby glanced at the clock and leaned forward. "Let me tell you something about Kimble. She is already separate from you, and there's not a damn thing you can do about it. You just described a mother of a certain class. Maybe to you it's the *them* class, but it's how Kimble was born to be raised. You just have to paint by the numbers. I think you knew this about her. I think it's what drew you to her." Libby glanced down for a moment. "I'm afraid we need to stop here."

She uncrossed her stockinged legs, and they fell apart more widely than she had anticipated. When she rose to show Meg out, she forgot which leg should dominate her stance. She nearly fell, then wobbled for what seemed an interminable time. All the while, Libby's gaze locked onto Meg's, and they both ignored the enfeeblement that would dominate their memory of the session, if they let it.

∞   ∞   ∞

For the first time, Meg had hired a baby-sitter for Kimble— Jeb, the 14-year-old stepson of Chris, the painter downstairs, the man who had hung prints of Christian history paintings all over the elevator.

"Meg-leg!" shouted Kimble the moment Meg unlocked the door. It was a new name discovered by Kimble three weeks before, when Meg had come upon a peg-leg pirate in a bedtime story. "Meg-leg, save me!"

"From what?" asked Meg, placing her keys in an asymmetrical pot she had held out of an order.

"Death and destruc, destruc-tion."

"Jeb, where did she learn that?"

"Megasis. We went downstairs to play. Dad said it was OK."

Is this what she would have to contend with? Meg wondered. Children baby-sitting children? Too bleary from her session with Libby, she spared Jeb a lecture on gratuitous violence and paid him to return downstairs. Then she made herself some coffee and settled down at the kitchen table to open her mail. She gave Kimble a Ho Ho and a glass of milk. From her backpack she removed the Dover book of the English royal family. She explained to Kimble that she was about to see the world's most dignified imperial family in its underwear. If she promised to use only her special blunt-nosed scissors, she would be able to dress them however she liked. Kimble's eyes grew wide at the prospect.

Meg tossed aside two identical fliers encouraging her to re-elect her state assemblyman. Beneath these was a postcard whose handwriting dislodged a fury of emotions—a thrill, a triumph, then a plunge to dread:

Dear Meg,

I'm coming in the second week in October to see a new client. I never thought I'd stoop to designing the packaging for The Savory Sachet Company, but there you have it. I'll be free on Tuesday night for dinner, and I'd love to see you. Maybe we can meet at The Blue Rooster at 7:00. You can just leave a message to confirm—we usually have the machine on.

I'd love to see you,
Sarina

The Blue Rooster, a small, lace-curtained restaurant on Eighth Avenue, had been gone for years. And for years Meg had been grateful not to have to pass it en route to her consignment shops in Chelsea. Although the restaurant had been a favorite of theirs, it was also the site of their breakup—right in front of the brick fireplace, right next to an antique hearth set. Meg remembered how she had placed herself in an Early American tableau immediately after Sarina told her she really thought it was time for them to move on. *Move on* is the term she had used, as if she were leading a cattle drive. Meg's gaze had fallen to the hearth set, and she had seen herself, in Quaker costume, pumping the bellows. At first she was unable to manage its awkward handles, but gradually (as Sarina delicately brought up the subject of who would take the cat) she had worked up such a voracious rhythm that the flames rose up and out of the fireplace, consuming the Blue Rooster and everyone in it. When the restaurant had finally shut down, Meg had asked around to see what happened, fully expecting to learn it had been destroyed by fire. As it turned out, the IRS had shut it down for nonpayment of back taxes.

For a month after that dinner at the Blue Rooster, Meg's attempts to rekindle Sarina's interest were wide and shameless. She suggested opening up their relationship. She wrote to Columbia's MBA program, thinking she would pursue a corporate career just long enough to buy Sarina her longed-for country house. Imagining herself a facile moneymaker, Meg had puffed around the apartment for a week trying on the swagger and spinning off the sports metaphors of the deal-maker. Sarina had just looked at her sadly as she packed her belongings and called the movers. In the end, Meg had resorted to an all-out character assault, accusing Sarina of shallowness, of fear of intimacy. ("Fear of intimacy," Libby had snapped years later when Meg described their breakup. "What's that? Have you been reading Dr. Cleo Cliché in *Glamour* magazine? The woman didn't want to be with you. What the hell is fear of intimacy?")

"Jesus, the Blue Rooster," muttered Meg now.

"What, Meg-leg?"

Meg looked up, surprised. "Nothing, honey. It's just the name of a restaurant. How are you doing there?"

"Fine."

"Very nice," said Meg, glancing at the cut-out dolls. "Beautiful." Kimble had affixed an ascot over Prince Charles's groin and a tiara at a jaunty angle on Princess Di's head. The rest of her remained unclothed.

"They're going out to dinner," Kimble confided.

"That's nice, honey. Did they make reservations?"

"What's that?"

"That's when you call ahead to a restaurant so they'll have a table waiting for you."

Kimble looked alarmed. "No! They didn't make reser-vaca-tions. They forgot!"

"Don't worry. We'll just call the Blue Rooster. Should I ask for a table for two or four? We might want to go too."

"Four! And I'm going to have six blue roosters."

Meg smiled and walked to her bedroom to call Sarina's machine. She gave her the address of a pasta place a block from the old Blue Rooster. When she returned Kimble had replaced Prince Charles's ascot with a pair of riding jodhpurs. She had dressed Princess Di in a Chanel suit. The tastefulness of these outfits so disappointed Meg that when Kimble held up the dolls she could only offer a weary nod. Kimble glared back at her, cold and exultant, as if she had for the first time glimpsed the competitive advantage of her conforming nature.

8

On a gusty Saturday afternoon the first week of October, Meg and Kimble stood and looked up at a vast apartment house, one of three of identical design, in Rego Park, Queens. Kimble declared she knew exactly which one was Grandma Shirl's, so Meg gathered her collar and hunched her shoulders against the wind as Kimble counted eight flights up and one balcony to the left of the apartment entrance. "That's it! That's my tricycle. Daddy bought me it, and then Grandma Shirl stole it and tol' everyone she bought it."

"Really? That's not just a story you're making up?"

"No. Chantelle tells stories all the time, and Tito sometimes does. But I never tell stories. This is my real truth."

Meg took Kimble's hand, and they made their way across the parking lot. People pay decent rents to live here, thought Meg. They like living here. It amazed her. Living in one of these Rego Park high-rises could only come from an impulse to snuff oneself out. But she knew these people probably spent more time on their apartments than she did on her loft, laying down pre-stick tiles, hanging pewter light fixtures, assembling home entertainment centers. It was all Meg could do to place one foot in front of the other to enter Shirley's building. There they passed a doorman at a freestanding counter on which was placed a basket of dried fall flowers. Inside the basket there was a tin plaque emblazoned with a verse called "Ode to Autumn." The doorman did not even look up from his racing forms as Meg and Kimble passed by.

This meeting had been confirmed twice. Shirley answered the door the moment Meg knocked. She had just been to the beauty parlor. Her hair was helmet-stiff.

"On time to the minute!" declared Shirley, pointing to her watch for Kimble's benefit. "How are you, angel?"

"Fine. Do you have Gummi Bear cupcakes?"

"Of course. Come in. Give me your coats. Let Meg get settled. Meg, I couldn't interest you in a Gummi Bear cupcake, could I?"

"No, thank you." Meg looked around in some dismay. She had not imagined this would be an efficiency apartment. She had imagined they would send Kimble into the bedroom to watch television. There was only one room, with a tiny sleeping alcove. The main room was dominated on one side by a heavy mahogany highboy. The doors were left open, and the shelves were filled with framed glossy photographs of the autumn woods.

"The Blue Ridge Mountains," said Shirley when she saw Meg looking. "My girlfriend sent them from her trip last year. I try to keep in touch with the seasons in here. I'm really a nature girl at heart."

"Uh-huh," said Meg. "Shirley, I think Kimble would like to watch television while we talk. Do you have a television?"

"Of course!" spluttered Shirley. "Do you think I'm un-American? Dollface, show Meg where my television is."

Kimble went up to another mahogany cabinet and pressed the top of a door. She smiled somewhat affectedly, thought Meg, when the door swung open to reveal a Sony with an out-size screen.

Meg had timed this visit to coincide with Kimble's favorite Saturday morning cartoons. Shirley switched on the television and went to get a cupcake from the kitchenette. When Kimble sat cross-legged on the floor her atomizer fell out of the pocket of her jumper. She patted it protectively, left it there beside her. Shirley returned. "So, we should talk," she said, as if the idea, the urgency, were hers.

The couch they sat on was a violet brocade, covered in sections by an afghan and several satin throw pillows. Meg rearranged the pillows to give herself room. Shirley put her feet on the coffee table and covered her legs with the afghan. "Bad circulation," she said, for the room was warm.

On the coffee table were some *People* magazines, an illustrated volume on glassblowing, and two well-worn Little Golden Books: *Peppy the Puppy* and *Sunday is Zoo Day.*

"I'm going to come directly to the point, Mrs. Marzola."

"Oh, for heaven's sake, honey, call me Shirley. How old are you, by the way?"

Meg blushed. It was true she was considerably past the age where she had to formally address her elders. By certain standards, she was herself an elder.

"Shirley, you know I didn't know Barry for very long, and I'm sorry I didn't know Anita at all. But I did know Barry at a crucial time. He told me a lot, and I believe everything he told me was stripped-down, straight from his heart." Meg lowered her voice to nearly a whisper. "After all, he was dying. He said…he suggested that you did not feel entirely comfortable with the idea of raising Kimble. Is that true?"

Shirley looked over at Kimble, who was hunched before the TV. "Dollbaby, don't sit so close. Your eyes are precious organs." With great effort she looked back at Meg. She cocked her head, said nothing. Her expression was inscrutable.

In the outside pocket of Meg's black leather backpack was the envelope from St. Luke's Hospital, the one that had been mailed to Meg after Barry's death. It contained the napkin on which he had scrawled his wishes. "This is to make it legel…" as if Barry could claim on the brink of death the authority he had lacked in life. Meg was glad she had the envelope, but she could not now imagine showing it to Shirley. In truth, it was a vehement last wish that Barry thought he could contort into a directive. She recrossed her legs. "I think Barry said the exact word you used was 'weary.' You were 'too weary to start all over again with a little girl.' Am I quoting right?"

"You're probably quoting exactly right, dear, but I wouldn't say that what I said then applies now. Things change, nothing ever stands still. To breathe is to change. Kimble is my daughter's daughter. My son-in-law, he was beneath mention, vermin from under a rock. But she is my daughter's daughter. What did you have in mind, dear?"

Meg had come to this meeting prepared for ugliness. She had talked to Honey in Barry's old building. She had found out that Shirley had taken off one day when Anita was eight years old, that she had just left her with a freezerload of TV dinners. She had sweet-talked the judge at family court into getting her back, then did the same thing again and again well into Anita's adolescence. "You don't have to be Einstein to figure out the convent," Honey had said. "Nobody gets abandoned in a convent. Stripped of worldly goods," she had snickered, "but never abandoned."

Meg was prepared to bring what she knew to light, to

squarely confront Shirley if necessary. But of the countless scenarios she had projected for this visit, it never occurred to her that Shirley Marzola would try to sell her granddaughter to Meg.

"Well, I didn't have anything in mind. I came here to see if Barry was right, if you don't feel up to raising Kimble. I guess I don't have to tell you that I've grown very attached to her over these last weeks. But of course, legally speaking, you have temporary custody."

"I can see you're attached," said Shirley. She cocked her head in Kimble's direction. "Our biological clocks are funny, aren't they? To breathe is to change; you can't foretell anything in this life. I might consider giving over custody. You'll excuse me for having to say this, but adoptions don't go cheap these days. Have you checked? They're not cheap at all, but when you think about it, why should they be? Human life is priceless. Still, I happen to think that someone like you should not be deprived of motherhood." Shirley looked at the cartoon on the television, a superhero ranting maniacally about revenge. She looked above Kimble's head. The little girl's hair was full of static electricity from the dry, overheated room. A fragile network of blond hairs stood comically on end. Shirley kept her eyes fixed on this strange nimbus.

Neither did Meg look at Shirley. She just nodded her head slowly and confided, "She's only been symptomatic for a month. But since we've started her on AZT her appetite's back to normal."

Shirley's gaze went from the cartoon to the atomizer, to the funny halo, back to the cartoon. She opened her mouth to speak, then closed it again. From the TV came the sound of gunfire, actually juju beans spraying from a blue coyote's rifle. Kimble was laughing.

Finally, Shirley turned to Meg. "Barry Toffler was on this

earth for 32 years, and he lied for just about all of them. Do you know what he told Anita when she met him? That he had a construction business that employed 20 people. She knew he'd been in prison, but do you know what she thought *for*? Because he had knocked down a man who was slapping up his wife on the street! He told Anita the man accidentally hit his head on a fire hydrant and died two days later. Barry said the wife refused to testify at his trial. Can you imagine? He lied about everything else, why shouldn't he lie about Kimble?" Shirley poked her elbow in Kimble's direction. "The man destroyed my whole family. Some people are pure, unadulterated evil from the moment they are born."

Over her years at REACH, how many times had Meg heard people describe others in the very words that best described themselves? It was as though they had a compulsion to utter the damning words, to fling them into their own orbit.

Shirley rested her head on the back of the couch and looked at the ceiling. "The fact is, I'm embarrassed to admit this at my age, but I've actually been seeing a man. You met him, come to think of it. Mr. Zito from Fanelli's? He's a widower with grown children, and, to be perfectly honest, he was never so hot on the idea of kids in the first place."

"Ow!" yelled Kimble from the floor. A leather-gloved fist dominated the television screen, then jagged multicolored streaks reached to all four corners.

"Maybe that's enough violence for this morning," said Meg.

Kimble walked up to the couch. She was wearing the tartan plaid jumper Meg had bought her. It was already getting small; her stomach strained against the front. "Can I have another Gummi Bear, Gran'ma Shirl?"

"I don't think so," intervened Meg. "All these sweets are getting out of control."

"Oh, but it's good for her to eat," interrupted Shirley. She disappeared into the kitchenette just long enough for Meg to lift Kimble to her lap, to pat down the funny little net of suspended hair and lay her hand on Kimble's head, an expiation that Meg silently granted herself. "You didn't hear that," she whispered. "No one in the world heard that." Kimble squirmed away the moment Shirley emerged with a full plate of cupcakes. Her arm, as well as her head and neck, strained toward the one whose sweep of pink frosting rose highest off the plate.

9

The following Saturday morning, Meg called Jeb again. "Forget it," he said. "Soccer."

Fourteen years old, thought Meg. "Uh-huh. Listen, hon, do you know someone else? One of your classmates who might want some extra cash?"

"Nah. No offense, but it's not all that interesting. I mean that Roller Queen shit really gets on your nerves after a while. Like she's obsessed. You could try Amanda Kroll from my second-period social studies. She's kind of a geek."

Not much of an endorsement, but Meg did not have the time—nor, apparently, the bait—to attract a higher-grade–baby-sitter. Jeb could not be expected to have memorized Amanda's number, but he told Meg she probably lived within a dozen blocks of them.

Amanda showed up on Duane Street three hours later.

"I'm going to my mother's, uptown," Meg explained. "I've put the number—"

"What's that?" Amanda pointed to one of Meg's pots, a gravy boat in the shape of a reclining naked woman, a portrait of Cami Porter lounging during the week they became lovers.

"A gravy boat."

"God. Really?"

Meg called Kimble, who emerged from the back in her Victorian print dress, a cardigan sweater, ankle socks ribbed with lace, and patent leather Mary Janes—all taken from the suitcase Honey had helped Meg to pack weeks before.

Amanda looked doubtful, as if Kimble's costume was some kind of a ruse. "You dressed up for me?" she asked. Then, to Meg, "She dresses like that?"

"She likes meeting new people," said Meg. She showed Amanda where Charlotte's number was next to the phone, then left.

∞   ∞   ∞

"It's so nice to be back among all my things," declared Charlotte as she swept open the door. Meg was jarred not so much by the statement as by the sleek lines of her mother's new Donna Karan, a black vest worn over a calf-length skirt slit up the side.

When Meg was growing up, Charlotte had worn prim woolen suits whose silk blouses had broad, ruffled collars. She had worn cashmere sweater sets and on summer evenings raw silk dresses with matching cloaks. Her complicated arrangement of french braids had been reassembled every few days at a hotel salon where for years she had had an account. Expertly wrapped and looped, these braids had given her the air of an exotic child. As a little girl, Meg noticed that her mother was somehow less adult-looking than other mothers. Yet the hairstyle was the perfect frame for her heart-shaped face.

Now Charlotte's silver-rinsed hair was razor-cut close to her head, like her friends'. She dressed like them too, in Armani and DKNY. But Ida Tree and the others had tough, leathery looks Charlotte did not share. While most of her friends seemed to have the high sunken cheeks and insouciant mouths of the worldly, Charlotte, at 73, had an expectant lilt in her voice. (Often her mother slipped into a doleful tone, but Meg did not trust it; she had once arrived at the Guggenheim right behind Charlotte, only to overhear her humming some Broadway tune, its lyrics devoted to romantic ambition.) Her hands and arms, too, divided her from her friends—women who pushed their Robert Morris bracelets over sharp wrist bones and up arms whose muscles were still sleek and ageless until a wrist turned to check the time on a watch. Then the skin of these women's forearms would stretch into a pattern of delicate and becoming wrinkles. In contrast, the skin of Charlotte's forearms was doughy. Her wrists were plump, and they had a tendency to fly up when she was dismayed or irritated, creating a band of deep creases. In another era her mother's type had worn wide-brimmed hats and dresses with flouncy skirts. Charlotte in smooth gabardine was a woman whose equilibrium had to be reinvented each morning.

"It was such a wonderful trip, I can't begin to tell you," she said before Meg was fully in the door. "I was so excited to show you these slides, I just ran to one of those one-hour places. How are you, dear? It's cold out, isn't it? I have some Rémy. Would you like to warm up?"

"That would be nice," said Meg, who rarely drank.

"I'll join you, and we'll get started right away. Then we'll talk. You'll indulge me this little rudeness, won't you? I'm just so thrilled!"

Charlotte had already loaded the carousel—a good thing, because Meg knew this would not be her mother's first glass of Rémy. Charlotte was a very peculiar kind of drinker. As far as

Meg knew, Charlotte drank on weekend afternoons only. During these allotted times she often drank liberally. This habit had always struck Meg as a game her mother played with herself, giving with one hand and taking away with the other. This afternoon her face had been flushed when she had answered the door. Now all she had to do was lie back on the couch, sip cognac, and click the remote control that advanced the carousel.

"Now, I've written everything down, so I'm all prepared," trilled Charlotte. "They may be a little out of order... oh, *look!*" On the screen appeared an unidentifiable reptile, bigger and fatter than a lizard, a spiky mane running the length of its neck and head.

"My God," said Meg. "It looks like a dinosaur descendant!"

"Yes! It really does. It's a marine iguana. To me it looks for all the world like a storybook dragon. Aren't the colors really something? That's the extraordinary part of the wildlife, the colors. They make all our animals look washed out by comparison."

Charlotte had arranged the slides not by island but by animal type. They went through a variety of marine and land iguanas, tortoises and turtles. One slide showed Ida and Juliet bending over on either side of a giant tortoise. Ida was aiming her camera at the tortoise's shell. Juliet examined the pattern of its thickly scaled front legs. Her suede sandal was poised next to the tortoise's muddy clubfoot.

"That's pretty funny." Meg took a sip of cognac.

Charlotte said nothing. She was clicking the advance to no avail. "What's wrong here?" she demanded.

As her mother got up to jiggle the carousel, Meg refocused on her objective for the afternoon. Her pulse quickened. The cognac and the exotic slides were taking her off with them. She could not remember exactly how she had planned to ask her mother. She had called Libby, and they had selected each word together. The words had added up to an elegant plea, but a plea just the same. Written down, these same words would mutate into the stuff of extortion.

"*Now* we're back in business. Birds! The birds, Meg...I cannot begin to describe them. This is a waved albatross. Ida and I saw it try to seduce another albatross. It twirls around and flaps its wings."

"That's subtle," said Meg. Just bide your time, she told herself. Make the tart remark she expects of you. Don't get distracted. Stay on course.

"Now here we are on the island of Hood, in the southeastern part of the Galapagos. This is the blue-footed booby that's so famous. This one waddled right up to Juliet! So many of the animals and birds took to her. She seems to have a rapport with wild creatures."

"I guess they're easier for her than domestic ones."

"Very amusing, Meg. This trip was just the thing for her. It gave her a whole new lease on life."

Meg nodded. "Sorry," she said. "I'm being glib." (Her nervousness was not abating. What was she supposed to say: "By the way, when were you planning to liquidate that Putnam Fund?" This was her mother. Some of her money might be thrown to Donna Karan, but some of it was her security. She could only hope it would be simply more designer clothes that her mother would sacrifice to help Meg with Kimble. Even at that, how could Meg ever know what these clothes, for which Charlotte had traded in her plausible style, really meant to her?)

"Should I show you the Charles Darwin Research Center, or should we save it for another time?" Her mother had slipped into the studied diction that gave her away as drunk.

When Meg did not immediately respond, Charlotte began to flick through the slides without pause.

"Stop, already!" Meg declared, but by that time Charlotte was already on to the luxury liner headed back to Quito. The slide she finally projected showed Ida and Juliet in the dining room, smiling on either end of an extravagant centerpiece of tropical fruits. Was this picture set up, wondered Meg, this mother and daughter whose mirrored expressions made Meg's skin crawl? How was she expected to react?

"You probably think this is a silly shot," acknowledged Charlotte.

"No, I don't," lied Meg.

Charlotte did not click ahead. Instead she called out the name of each kind of fruit in the pyramid. She described its color and texture and compared its taste to that of other fruits. This was a time-consuming task during which Meg had no choice but to gaze at the vapid, beaming faces of Ida and Juliet, in love with their kind and with each other.

"It looks like a nice ship," said Meg. She poured some more Rémy, though its taste burned in her throat.

"It was, but not nearly as grand as the one your father and I took to the Virgin Islands that time." Click. The slide showed her mother's stateroom. A dressing table was neatly wedged between two built-in wardrobes. "That was a ship to surpass all ships. They'll never build one like that again. Marble columns in the dining room, mahogany paneling in the staterooms."

The trip to the Virgin Islands when Meg was eight was the only vacation she remembered her parents taking together. The explanation that had come down to Meg was that Steven was married to his work. Charlotte had called him an empire builder, and her pleasure in saying this had been obvious. Meg herself had been proud. Steven manufactured billing equipment that was shipped all over the world. If all her father's noisy printing machines had seemed unrelated to the glory of the Roman Empire, which Meg had read about in a picture book, she guessed it was the fault of her fragmentary understanding of the world.

"Now where exactly did you go on that trip?" Meg asked.

"Oh, you know, all those 'Saint' islands. It was nothing much. Nothing at all like this trip."

"But how did you get him to go? You two didn't take trips."

"That was the only thing that separated me from my girl-friends," said Charlotte. "They traveled with their husbands; I traveled with you. Not that I didn't love traveling with you—you were such a little mischief-maker. Remember that time in Portugal when you got locked in the hotel room?"

Meg remembered the trip but not this episode that Charlotte always brought up. What she recalled was shellfish that made her sick and her mother complaining that the Madeira linen was more expensive than in Lord & Taylor.

"Well, I guess if Daddy had gone, I wouldn't have, so I have no complaints," said Meg. "But how *did* you get him to go that time?"

"Oh..." said Charlotte, her voice trailing.

Meg waited.

"I don't consider that trip a particular coup," her mother admitted.

"Because?"

"Meg, you're in therapy, aren't you?"

Not once had Meg ever alluded to Libby. "So?" she accused, a knee-jerk challenge, a child's retort. She was immediately ashamed.

"I thought so. I'm not judging. I'm sure your life is not without its complications. But your being in therapy doesn't mean everyone around you has to plumb the deep fathoms."

"For Christ's sake, Mom! I'm not asking you to plumb anything." The slide of the stateroom still dominated the opposite
wall. Meg stared angrily at the collection of Lancôme cosmetics laid out just as they were on her mother's dressing
table at home.

Charlotte, too, kept her attention on the slide. "Your father
agreed to take that trip with me supposedly to get away from a
woman. He didn't want to marry her; he wanted to stay married
to me, but he didn't want to give her up. This is not a new story.
You may not have heard it from me, but I don't have one friend
without a similar story."

Meg recrossed her legs and sat back on the stiff love seat.
She would not let Charlotte think she was luring her into the
depths. "Similar, but different too, I'm sure," she remarked
neutrally.

"There are some differences." Charlotte's lipstick had worn
away. Her lips were pale and lined, the corners receding into
faint shadows. For a moment Meg wished her mother would go
into the half-bathroom off the foyer and come back renewed,
lines smooth, colors luminescent—a young heroine from a '30s
movie, a coquette bound to detain her roaming husband.

"Do you and your friends talk? Do you compare your different stories?"

"Honey," snapped Charlotte, "maybe you sit around with
your friends, from that REACH or wherever, and discuss and
analyze. That's fine if it's important to you, but I'm certain my
friends would get no satisfaction out of me humiliating myself
in a *session* of some kind."

"I'm not talking about humiliation! That's not what this is
about."

"Meg, can we just stop this, please?"

"You were the one who brought up the Virgin Islands." Meg could not bear her own peevish tone.

"I just invited you over to show you my slides, to share my slides. I thought you'd be interested...you have an interest in new places. Why does it always have to escalate into some emotional scene?"

"Do I seem emotional?" asked Meg, holding open her palms as if to prove her equanimity.

"I'll tell you what was different about my story, if that will make you happy. The difference was that your father consented to go with me to the Virgin Islands, but he had already flown the woman down to St. Croix, and she was waiting for him at a hotel by the time we disembarked. She didn't know I'd be there, and I didn't know she'd be there."

Absently, Charlotte clicked ahead to the next slide, a view of the ship's gift shop.

"What a fucking misogynist," said Meg.

"Reduce, reduce," chanted her mother.

"So what happened?"

Charlotte sucked on her cheek, inclined her head toward the ceiling. "We both stayed, and we both heard about each other for years. Steven chose to confide in me. What she had that I didn't. It was taken for granted that this kind of talk would not jeopardize his position with me. I can't imagine what he told her about me, but I'm certain it was not an inventory of my merits. Your father always let me know I would be taken care of after he was gone, while she would not be. I have no idea how this arrangement served him. She died about five years ago, and the circumstances were not good, as I'm told. So the differences between your era and mine are really quite pronounced, aren't they?"

Meg could not take her eyes off her mother, her features so

bleary above the fitted black vest. What should she do or say? Charlotte had made a lifelong habit of riding the surface. Over and over Meg had complained to Libby that she didn't know the least thing about her mother's life, that it was unnatural how little she knew, and now, inside of five minutes, Meg suddenly knew things. "That's quite a story," she remarked—*sang*, to her horror, her voice rising determinedly just as Charlotte's own voice tended to soar above the site of bare facts.

"Yes, but you'd be surprised how common it is, or some version of it. Ida's husband stopped her checks on their joint account. He gave her an allowance and made her beg for it every time. You should be glad you're in a different era, and maybe you should be glad…" At this moment, Charlotte's face sagged so much that Meg realized her mother generally avoided lowering her head. "Would you like another Rémy?"

"No. Thanks. I really need to get going. I left Kimble with a sitter."

"Kimble! Listen to how I've gone on, right as there are probably things you're bursting to tell me about that little girl." Charlotte straightened in her chair.

If she had the time, Meg told herself, she would stay the night—something she had never done—and they would keep talking until color bloomed on Charlotte's cheeks and she began to hum hopeful little show tunes. But Meg was late. She rose from her seat right as the next slide jumped to the screen. It showed a row of blue-footed boobies from the cruise liner's gift shop—bubble bath, according to a sign. Molded smiles demeaned them, yet miles away the real seabirds were also called upon to cleanse, to waddle up to shiploads of beleaguered Americans seeking renewal.

"I got one of those for Kimble," Charlotte remembered. "Let me go find it."

Her mother was gone a long time, and Meg thought about her father and the woman in St. Croix. What parting words could she possibly offer that would mean anything, that would console? Would they talk about it next time? Never mention it again? Who would make the decision, Meg or Charlotte?

"Here it is!" Charlotte declared, her face now remade. "I have a present for you too, but it's dug somewhere under my things."

"I'll get it next time," said Meg, taking the blue-footed booby. She hugged her mother, all the while keeping her eyes on the gift shop, with its bubble bath, its plush albatrosses, its rows of postcards flaunting the turquoise water off the Galapagos Islands.

∞   ∞   ∞

Black surfaces slashed across Meg's view as she rushed through the loft. The TV screen, the Mission chair with its leather cushions and kilim pillows, many of the pots on Meg's drying racks, a Shaker cabinet with glass doors—all were covered with streaks of black. The paint was only tempera, but its dull, pasty surface stabbed at Meg; wherever it touched, no light penetrated, no light was reflected.

"Amanda!" called Meg. "Amanda, where the hell are you?!"

There was no answer.

Meg picked up speed, then stopped in the middle of the floor and waited for a sound. "Amanda! Kimmy! *Answer* me!"

There came only a distant tapping. Meg followed its sound to the rear of the loft. There was Kimble faceup on top of the futon. Bunched at her feet, the Tinkerbell quilt was spattered with black paint. She stared at the ceiling. In her hand was a wet paintbrush which she swatted on the floor beside her. Nearby was a larger brush, black paint already dry on its bristles. Her breathing was labored, but she did not gasp for air. Meg took an atomizer from her backpack and held it in front of Kimble's mouth. Her lips readily opened, an infant's before a nipple. Meg's sense of relief was so physical it left her momentarily dopey. Kimble inhaled once, then just looked at Meg.

"What happened? Where's Amanda?"

"She's not here."

"I know she's not here, Kimble. Where is she?"

"She left to go home." Kimble lifted her arm and swiped at her cheeks with the paintbrush.

Meg grasped her wrist. "Listen to me. I don't know what happened to Amanda, but she was extremely bad to leave like this. Do you understand? Baby-sitters do not leave children under any circumstances."

"Ow!" cried Kimble. "You're hurting me."

Meg let go. Kimble flipped over on her stomach and thrashed her bare feet among the folds of the quilt. She still wore her print dress and cardigan. She tried to cry, but her voice was depleted.

"Who did all this painting?"

" 'Manda."

"Kimble...is that your real truth?"

"Yes."

"Why would Amanda do this? Why would she paint everything black?"

"She must hate everything."

"Forget Amanda. Do you hate everything?"

"Not Roller Queen. I didn't—I mean, 'Manda didn't paint Roller Queen."

"There is a tremendous amount of destruction in this room,

Kimble. It's going to take days to get this paint off. And my pots might be ruined."

"I hate your pots."

"What don't you hate?"

"I told you. Roller Queen."

"Ah, yes. Roller Queen, Roller Queen. Can I lie down with you?"

"I don't care." Kimble's eyes glazed with tears. Beneath the jagged black streaks her cheeks were mottled as if her blood twinkled inside her slender veins, never passing color evenly over her skin.

"You didn't ruin the Kimble pot, I noticed." Meg removed her backpack and lay down on the futon. Kimble did not move, but neither did she turn her face away from Meg. Her breathing was shallow now.

"I'm saving it. For Daddy."

Meg just lay there and listened to their breathing, inhales and exhales pitched to a counterpoint. Finally she said, "Your daddy's not coming back. I know you know this. Do you think you can try not to be afraid?" An involuntary hush emphasized her words.

"I'm not afraid!" protested Kimble, her ribs vibrating against Meg's. "I hate everybody. Everybody has AIDS and hates everybody else, and then everybody dies."

"What did Amanda tell you?"

"She said she knows Daddy died. She said she was sorry."

"Is that bad?"

"It's not her business!"

"You're probably right. But I don't think she said a bad thing, Kimmy. She *did* a bad thing, she did a very bad thing by leaving here, but that was not a bad thing she said."

"When does Daddy turn into a flower?"

Meg listened to the soft, idle thump of Kimble flicking the paintbrush against the wooden floor.

"Is that what Amanda said? That your daddy would turn into a flower?" Meg tried to keep her tone even, but once again she felt a sense of alarm at the myriad points of view to which a child is exposed. This latest one from Amanda sounded to Meg suspiciously informed by Fundamentalism.

"Yes. I'm going to put him into the Kimble pot. When he turns into a flower."

Meg picked up Kimble's hand. Her tiny hand was dead weight; it bore no strength, exercised no grip. Her nails were pink as her fingertips. Flakes of tempera paint curled off her palm. As much as Meg tried to concentrate on the moment, on Kimble and what she had done, she looked instead at this paint-covered little hand and remembered how long it had been since she had focused like this on a lover's hand, a comely hand that knew things, a grown-up hand that signaled the considerable things it knew. People dying of AIDS and becoming flowers. This was a notion she wanted to turn over with an adult, someone who would know to relegate it to the flaccid piety it was, someone who had a little perspective.

"Kimmy, listen to me. You know how Kevin from the playroom has stayed with his Aunt Gwyn for a long time?"

"Yes. Because he doesn't have AIDS, but his mother does. But his Aunt Gwyn doesn't."

"That's right." In point of fact, Kevin's mother was blind from CMV and would probably be dead within a month. His aunt was already making arrangements to adopt him. "That's right, and you've been staying with me sort of like Kevin stays with his Aunt Gwyn."

"But you're not my aunt."

"True, I'm not, because I'm not related to you by blood."

Kimble looked at Meg. "That's good, because then if you were, you could get AIDS."

It had never occurred to Meg until this moment that a four-and-a-half-year-old had assumptions about who she was in the world. Kimble assumed herself to be a danger. She thought people were lucky not to be related to her. In Kimble's mind, Meg needed to be protected from her. It was this antic reversal of their roles that made Meg see that in the years to come their connection would sometimes be unbearable. Despite Libby's faith that Meg would use Kimble's origins as the bedrock of their separateness, the two of them had begun to silently wrangle over who would be sturdy, who would be fragile.

Meg smoothed back Kimble's hair. Paint stuck in clumps across her hairline. "You know that I'm not going to get AIDS. Ever. But listen to me now. Soon Kevin is going to move in with his Aunt Gwyn, and she'll be the one to take care of him all the time."

"Because his mother's going to die from AIDS?" asked Kimble. She took away her hand and started to peel the tempera off her palm.

"Yes. I'm afraid that's right. But Kevin's Aunt Gwyn is a fine lady, and I think Kevin is going to be happy living with her."

Meg waited for Kimble to draw a parallel with her own circumstance. She may as well have told her straight-out: Abandoned children can be reclaimed by fine ladies. Kimble said nothing, just rubbed her hands together so that twists of dried black paint showered onto the Tinkerbell sheets. Then she sat up and asked, "Can Kevin come over tomorrow?"

Meg tickled Kimble in the ribs. "You don't even like him. He called you a baboon, remember?"

"No!" shouted Kimble, joyful.

Meg placed a finger over Kimble's lips and said, "Now I

have a serious question. Have you ever seen a blue-footed booby filled with bubble bath?" She got up and took the gift bottle from her bag.

"What is it?" breathed Kimble.

"It comes all the way from the Galapagos, enchanted islands in the Pacific Ocean. Here, look inside." Meg unscrewed the cap and let Kimble look at the pink liquid that rose to the top of the bird's plastic neck. "We're taking him into the bathtub right now, and then I'm going to call Amanda's parents and say many swear words over the phone. You could listen, if you want. But I want you to know that if you ever open that paint again and put it on anything other than paper…"

But Kimble had already jumped up and was running toward the bathroom, discarding first her cardigan, then her imitation Laura Ashley, then a velveteen bow all puckered under dense clots of black paint.

10

The offices of REACH and of the Child Welfare Administration were worlds apart. To Meg, the difference was clear illustration of what happens when an emergency commutes over time into a state of persistent need. REACH was private and still young. Broad-minded philanthropists had invested hundreds of thousands. They still invested. The richest members of the gay community had given generous sums every few months—magical thinking on designer checks. Some of them survived to continue writing checks. Luxurious materials had been donated: A top design firm had come forward with sconces, milky glass fans in a different hue for each of the five floors. One hundred and fifty in all. The walls were painted in coordinating tones of gray and plum gloss. The editor of an architecture magazine, now two years dead, had furnished seven conference rooms with soft leather couches. At Christmastime, select door frames were strewn with evergreen and tiny white, always white, lights. The funds had poured in. Money still flowed. An emergency bedecked in the finest of everything. And why not, many had argued. Some had answered that it was unseemly. They pointed to other agencies, Human Resources and its Child Welfare Administration. Settings of epidemics grown sustainable, these agencies had never been flush. People regarded them as necessary evils, and no one left their doors uplifted. Money will make the difference, the management of REACH insisted. (And when it doesn't, sniped a volunteer, at least the brunches will be pleasant.) Meg knew only that on the day she went directly from REACH to Child Welfare, two days after Kimble's painting rampage, she descended so many tiers of compromise that it was all she could do not to turn heel and run home.

At REACH Meg had dropped Kimble off in the playroom and went up to her 11 o'clock appointment with Tina. A perennially flushed chemical blond, Tina greeted all of her long-term volunteers with a big hug. She was a woman entirely suited to her job. Her work hours were fueled by pumped-up adrenaline. She galloped to the wellspring of every crisis, wrung her hands and made solicitous calls to waiting-list clients when emergencies were in abeyance. The zealousness of her giving was purely missionary. It was said she was a devout Catholic-turned-atheist and could not stop putting out for others. She lived humbly, in a dingy alcove studio on the Upper West Side, but claimed that her life of privilege obliged her to do for the less fortunate. She made no such demands on people far better off than she.

Tina was famous for not identifying her sexual orientation. Over the years she had hinted at women, intimated men, and in the dead of winter made jokes about Ding-Dong, her overweight schnauzer. She was grounded in middle age, but guesses ran the gamut from 30 to 50. The fierce drive behind her nurturing had put off some novice volunteers, while it had sustained older ones. Yet Tina's charged merriment did not mask her inability to really get down with people, to shed her exalted ideals and fill her own plate. Meg had met with Tina many times over the years but had always felt, beneath the exuberant welcome, a trace of scorn.

"Sit down, hon," boomed Tina once Meg was inside her carpet-paneled cubicle. "We haven't talked in—I don't know, it seems like forever. How many weeks? Not to pressure you that we have 80 clients on our waiting list and you're one of our most experienced volunteers. Not in the slightest," she trilled, "because you deserve a little sabbatical now and then. Oh, yes, however long you need, I'm here to care for the caretakers, my shoulder exists for your comfort, but *please*," she laughed, "just tell me you're ready for another client starting yesterday. Here," she pushed forward a box of Russell Stover chocolates, "have one. They're from a client's grateful mother, so we don't hold her accountable for her taste. How *are* you, hon?"

Meg smiled weakly. All that was on her mind was her cover-up to Tina weeks before; she had never been at ease with subterfuge. When she was six years old, just a year and a half older than Kimble, she had pulled off her first deception. It had been Camera Day at the Westchester Club, where she was enrolled in day camp. Steven had decided to lend her his Nikon. Meg had understood the gesture to signify his growing trust in her maturity. He had shown her how to work the automatic light meter and press the shutter button. Then he had said, "I'm entrusting you with a top-of-the-line piece of equipment." He had looked solemn, and so had Charlotte. Standing at the corner, awaiting the camp bus that would take Meg to Westchester, Charlotte had cautioned Meg to keep the lens cap in place until she was ready to shoot a photograph; she could not under any circumstances press the shutter button until she got to camp. On the bus Meg had removed the camera from its

stiff leather case to inspect its grainy surface, its chrome buttons and triggers, the multicolored little numbers on the ring at
the base of its lens. The more features she failed to identify, the
more she panicked. She could not even remember which button got the light meter to work and where she was supposed to
look to find the vibrating little pointer her father had shown her.
Deep into her inspection Meg's finger had slipped, or was
moved by some perverse curiosity, over the shutter release. A
deep click had resounded throughout the bus. Suddenly, she
had not been able to remember what her parents told her would
be the consequences of this accident. By the time the bus
arrived at camp, Meg was convinced that the camera was now
capable of exploding and that the Nikon people, who through
some sixth sense already knew of her transgression, could put
her in jail. She had refused to take a picture all day. At home
that night, Meg had returned Steven's Nikon and told him it
had turned out not to be Camera Day after all. Ever after, a
spectral dread had accompanied all her attempts at deception.

Weeks ago, when Meg had reported to REACH that
Kimble had gone back to Shirley Marzola, her heart had raced
as if she had just clicked that forbidden shutter release.

"I'm fine," she answered Tina now, "but I made this
appointment to tell you something important. Remember when
I said that Barry Toffler's mother-in-law had taken temporary
custody of Kimble?"

"Yes-s-s…" Tina nodded warily.

"All of that was true. But I have to tell you, Tina, it was an
incomplete story I was telling you. I mean, yes, the grandmother signed temporary-custody papers in the hospital when Barry
was in a coma. And Kimble went home with her. But the truth
is…she's with me again now."

Tina had just put a double-dark chocolate shell into her

mouth. Now she took a Kleenex from the dispenser next to her computer and spat the candy into it. She looked into its center. "I hate coconut," she said in a neutral voice. "Go on. I'm listening."

Meg laughed nervously. "See, this is what you guys get for sitting on those bylaws for a year and a half."

Tina just looked at Meg. Meg decided she was close to 50 after all. Her usual laughter and mugging obscured the deep fret lines Meg noticed this morning.

"Meg, I can't believe this is you. This is not funny. You know how serious this is. Tell me what happened."

"Remember before Barry Toffler died, when he was in the hospital, and you couldn't find the grandmother? Well, it turned out that she won some money in Atlantic City and took her friends to Palm Beach. When she came back I got hold of her, and she went to St. Luke's social services to sign the temporary-custody papers. The social worker did what she was supposed to do, and everything was set. But a few days later the grandmother called me to take Kimble again. Basically, she doesn't give a flying fuck."

"So after all this time Kimble is still with you?"

"Yes. I've been taking care of her." This last was said in an irresolute tone, a tone so faint it could have been exhumed from Camera Day.

Several people passed briskly by Tina's cubicle. She lowered her voice, clear signal for Meg to do the same. She tapped the index finger of her right hand against the wrist bone of her left. "And have you called the city? Do they know what's going on? They have to investigate the grandmother. If she's incompetent, Kimble would be put in foster care. Eventually she'd be handled by Leake and Watts. Or Harlem Dowling. Perfectly decent adoption agencies."

Before Meg could answer, Tina excused herself. When she came back she led Meg into an empty conference room and closed the door. In the past, Tina had insisted that Meg sit on the capacious leather sofa. This morning she sprawled over the length of it, shaking her leg as she waited for Meg to sit. Meg chose a cane-seated chair pushed up against the wall.

"Do you have any idea what a powder keg you're sitting on—excuse me, no, REACH is now sitting on with you? If our legal department knew this, it would be bad. Really bad. Let me tell you something, Meg. Two weeks ago a client on the waiting list asked if our volunteers were bonded. We thought it was pretty funny. For days we were walking around saying: 'Excuse me? Are our volunteers into bondage?' I don't think his question is so funny now, Meg." Tina dropped her head to rub her temples. Meg looked at her light-brown roots and the pink scalp of her part. "Meg, you've been a great volunteer. You know the rules, and if you didn't know them, you could intuit them, they're such common sense."

For these past seven years, Meg had shrugged modestly each time she had heard the inevitable "I don't know how you do it" or "I could never do that kind of work. I really admire you." Sitting in the conference room with Tina, staring at the cloudy glass bricks that separated them from the hall, Meg saw that her incentive to volunteer had never been honorable in the least. On some level, she had imagined that doing for others carried with it a special impunity. The reprisals meted out in the real world, Steven and Charlotte's world, somehow did not extend to volunteers for the common good. And so Meg had felt more independent at REACH than she had even at the potters workshop where she trained and later taught, certainly more independent than in any office job she had held in the years before her business took off. Volunteering had enabled her to answer questions with confidence, to comfort with no muddled expectations, to feel a swell of confidence each time she did the right thing in an emergency. There was a loftiness behind Meg's volunteering, and she saw it now, as if all these years she had merely looked at unimaginable misery, looked like a voyeur who could walk away, transformed yet unaccountable.

"I'm fired, aren't I?" Meg asked Tina.

"I don't know. The department has to talk. Probably. But beyond that, I'm going back to my office and calling the city."

"Tina, the reason I waited so long to tell you this is I'm going to try to adopt Kimble. This is not just a whim."

Meg saw that Tina was weeping. Oddly, her face was not red now. It was unusual for Tina to hold her face so still, to be so pensive. "I know you felt you were in a bind, but you should've called us. You can't adopt now. Not after what's happened…."

"Jesus!" burst out Meg. "You're going to go to the city and tell them about this? What I did might have been negligent, stupid even, but if you go to the city and doom this child to some horrible foster home—"

"They're not all horrible. Not at all."

"Uh-huh. I can send her to college, Tina. She's had an unspeakable start to her life, but I can send her to college."

Tina sat up and folded her hands in her lap. She blinked. Meg saw that she trembled. "Go downstairs to Ray. He has contacts at Child Welfare. If there's someone there who will give you a break, who will advocate for you, Ray will know who that person is. I never thought I'd have to talk to you this way, Meg, you of all people, but I have to tell you I am obligated to call CWA myself. Because it's you, honey, and because you've helped so many clients over the years, I will give you one day to work this out, to try to get the support you need. But you should know that tomorrow I am going to call CWA to make sure Kimble is in the system. We are accountable to the state, and if this gets out…well, it would be devastating for the agency. So, there's no need to fire you, right? We agree that you're resigning. Tit for tat. Go downstairs and talk to Ray."

Before Meg could respond, Tina stood up and held open the conference room door. As soon as they were in the hallway a volunteer who everyone called The Stockbroker With a Heart ran up to embrace Tina.

"Hi, hon!" Tina burst out, warmth returning to her voice, the signature flush spreading over her cheeks. "Wait for me in my cube. I have to go barf up some chintzy chocolates from a client's mom. *This* is how they thank us. Give me strength."

She left Meg standing in the middle of the hall.

∞   ∞   ∞

"Ray *Sun* Ray! Ray *Sting* Ray!" called the group of children gathered around the playroom supervisor.

"Ray *Fae* Wray," contributed Ray in a droll tone, smiling at Meg as she entered the basement room.

By now the children's faces were familiar to Meg: Jackie, Tito, Kevin, Pauly, Chantelle. Like Kimble, she kept a mental inventory: yes, yes, no, yes, yes.

"Kevin *Heaven* Kevin!" shouted Pauly.

"I'm going to heaven," said Jackie. "Our deacon said."

"Kevin's not going to heaven," offered Tito. "He's going to hell."

"You guys need to stop this and start being nice," said Ray. "It's never too late to start being nice. Kimble, there's Meg."

"Meg-*leg* Meg!"

Six children playing a game, thought Meg. Six children with too much sugar in their systems, who have only each other to vanquish. Two days earlier Kimble had painted half of Meg's loft with black tempera. Paint that could have been tar. Who knew what the other five children had done that Saturday, children who had nothing to lose at any hour of the day.

"I win!" shouted Kimble. "I win with Meg-leg Meg."

"I don't know how you do it," Meg said to Ray now. She had found it difficult enough to care for just one child. Yet focusing on Kimble, rosy-cheeked this morning and claiming Meg as hers, Meg felt a nearly shameful pride, as if Kimble were an egg baby she had managed to safeguard from the dangerous surfaces of the world. Meg well remembered the exercise of Trixie the Egg Baby because it had put into motion her transfer from public school on Manhattan's Upper East Side to private school in Riverdale. Trixie had become her charge in a home-economics class at the end of sixth grade. The unit for the month had been baby care. Each girl had been given an egg she was expected to name, bathe, and take with her everywhere she went for a week. To do this without breaking her egg, Meg needed to provide for its security during class, extracurricular activities, and evening outings. The purpose of the exercise was to prove the difficulty of safely ushering even a silent egg through life. Naming the egg personalized it. Dropping the named egg made grief palpable. Nineteen out of 26 girls managed to break their eggs before the week was out. Some had smashed theirs, throwing them from apartment or taxicab windows. Meg had preserved Trixie. Rather than recoil from the hardships of unplanned parenthood, Meg had clung to Trixie well beyond the term of the assignment. The Krantz family had been as alarmed by Trixie's name as by the realization that Meg's classmates were all unwed mothers *in potentia*. Steven had made a show of scrambling Trixie into a ceramic bowl for his Saturday omelette. The next semester Meg found herself in a wainscoted auditorium in Riverdale, listening to herself being described as one of tomorrow's achieving women.

"Oh, it's not hard," said Ray now. "I just take Xanax, Prozac, and Quaaludes in equal parts. My doctor is *very* sympathetic."

Meg laughed. She had heard Ray's doctor was also his lover. "I wonder if you could break away for a few minutes. I need to talk with you."

Ray looked at her. "Sure." He picked up the beeper he wore on his belt buckle. REACH had a buddy system within the agency as well as outside it. If a staff person needed assistance dealing with a client, several floaters were on call to come to the rescue. Meg thanked Ray, then frowned, trying to remember if Tina had been wearing her beeper today. Five minutes later a short man Meg had seen once or twice in Recreation appeared at the door of the playroom. Meg smiled at him. So did Ray. "Hi, Bill. Now, this is only an emergency," he said, "if you believe you can die from happiness." And in fact, all six children were now doing somersaults on the air mattresses meant for nap time. They had unplugged all the air valves, and now broke up in laughter each time a hissing sound was released.

"How lovely of you to have me," said Bill.

"The pleasure is all mine," Ray called back as he guided Meg out the playroom door. "I owe you."

∞   ∞   ∞

At the Atlantis Coffee Shop on Eighth Avenue, Meg ordered an herbal tea and asked Ray how he was.

He answered with a wave of his hand. "Keeping on," he said. "So what's up?"

"It's about Kimble. You know her father died, right?"

"Yes. The grandmother has temporary custody, was the last I heard. Although I can't tell you I haven't wondered what's going on with you, Meg. I mean, I know this is your first peeds client, but I'm surprised they haven't gotten on you about closure. Don't you just love that word? *Closure*. I've never had closure in one relationship in my life. Maybe now that I'm fading, I should buzz around town all day embarrassing the hell out of people I haven't seen in years. 'Sorry,' I'll say, 'but I can't get into paradise until I have *closure*.'"

Meg laughed. She wished she'd had Ray to call when her friends said her problem with Sarina was that she'd never had closure.

The waiter returned and put a tea before Meg and a chocolate milkshake before Ray. Meg blinked. "I saw you on television the other night. Channel 5 News."

"Yeah, everyone saw it. Who would've guessed these willowy limbs could scale a ten-foot fence?"

Along with others, Ray had been apprehended trying to break into the executive offices of a pharmaceutical company in New Jersey. They had gone beyond their planned civil disobedience and had spent some time in jail.

"It's great what you're doing, Ray. I'm behind you 100 percent. Actually, I'm pulling a little disobedience of my own, but I think it's gotten a bit out of control."

Ray stuck a straw in his milkshake and stirred a clump of ice cream. "I hate it when they don't mix it. I know the ones at McDonald's are gelatin and chemicals, but at least everything's no muss, no fuss. So...how can I help you?"

"Kimble's grandmother's out of the picture. She's been

totally negligent. She just doesn't want her. I've had Kimble almost all this time, but, of course, I don't have anything approaching legal custody."

"I can give you the number to call. It's an 800 number. A special child welfare number. You call it, and the judge gives custody to the state. I mean, first they'll have to do an emergency evaluation of the grandmother. But if it's clear that she's negligent, that she abandoned Kimble like you said, the judge will give custody. They don't like to fool around in these cases."

"Then what happens?" asked Meg.

"It depends. Probably family court will put Kimble in 90-day emergency placement."

"A foster home?"

"Most likely. What's the problem with the grandmother, anyway?"

"I wish I could tell you. You must see this awful stuff all the time. All I know is that she's getting married, and her boyfriend doesn't want Kimble either. It's mind-boggling."

Ray nodded.

"What if I just didn't call the 800 number? What if no one did?" Given the conversation Meg had just had with Tina, this question was purely hypothetical. Yet its recklessness gave her a sense of satisfaction.

"Meg, come on. The Child Welfare system might be Byzantine, but you can't get around it. What about when she starts school? What happens when it's time for her to get a Social Security number? What about a million things? No one can get legal guardianship without going through the system. Is that what you want, guardianship? Believe me, I'm the first to just take what I'm entitled to, but there may be some question here about entitlement. In their eyes, I mean."

"More than a little question, Ray. I've already had Kimble for weeks without reporting her." Meg took out her tea bag, wrapped it in half a napkin, and placed it in an empty ashtray. "Do you know anyone at Child Welfare?"

"You're really focused on this thing, aren't you?"

"Completely."

"Are you going to do this with benefit of partner?" Growing oddly detached, Ray used the same tone as when he had said "Ray. Fae Wray." He propped his elbow on his wrist and flicked at the rhinestone string that dangled from his left ear.

"I'm doing this with benefit of wanting to do it, which is not always the case, as you well know." Meg was aware that her voice, too, rose to a stereotypically tough inflection as she grew agitated. When she heard her defensive tone, she turned to look out the window at Eighth Avenue. It did not take much to deduce that Ray, who was gifted with children, might have wished to be a father. "I'm sorry, Ray. I'm being really jumpy. It took me a while to decide that this was something I wanted to do and could do, and now that I've decided, I think I might have already sabotaged it."

Ray sat whirling ice cream around the inside of his glass. Tender with children, exacting with adults, thought Meg. Perfect. She waited.

"I do know someone I really respect at Child Welfare. Her name is Consuela Soto. She can't bypass anything, but she can probably rush things for you." Ray stopped talking and tried to smile. Whether from pain or despair, his mouth quivered and settled on a shape that carried no detectable emotion, a shape that was bleary and diffident and entirely unreflective of Ray on any decent morning.

Meg in her volunteer role would have reached out to clasp his wrist, would have told him they could continue their talk some other time. As of this morning no longer a volunteer, she said, "Yes, please, let's go back and call Consuela."

∞   ∞   ∞

The only available seat was a broken orange fiberglass one, part of a row of identical chairs. Meg lowered Kimble onto it. Worn-out, Kimble stirred and dropped her head against her left shoulder. Her mouth drifted open, and her chest rose and fell heavily under her cardigan. She became as one with the children around her napping or stirring restlessly or playing on the floor. Some of these children wore tiny gold earrings and crosses around their necks. All appeared exhausted, as if they were personally managing the effort to place themselves into benevolent custody. Adults turned pages of newspapers and retrieved fallen bottles and toys. Most of the noise came from babies and children, a constant pitch of random sound, of statical discontent. Meg tried to center herself by reading *The New York Times*. She had been ashamed for years of having avoided the bureaucratic indignities others suffered daily, yet now she wanted out. She wondered if aesthetic deprivation alone could spawn violence. The room was dull and dirty and unventilated; in the corner stood a dead plant wrapped with a gold gift bow. Everyone waited to speak with a caseworker, and although Ray had made his call and received this special favor, it was clear the wait would be long.

All week Meg had avoided being alone with herself. Now Kimble was asleep, and the paper did not hold Meg's attention. Everywhere she turned for peaceful contemplation, she wanted to turn away. Against her will, she began to wonder about tomorrow night, when she would meet Sarina near the old Blue Rooster. Whatever was to emerge from that dinner, it would not be, as Ray would have it, closure. On the contrary, Meg had never been in a situation with an ex-lover that did not at some juncture forecast the possibility of beginning anew. For that reason, she usually avoided meeting old lovers. Last week Cami had left a message on her machine, and Meg had not returned the call. Experience had taught her not to embroider on the single rush of attraction that invariably loomed during wine-filled evenings. Experience had proved that trying to make much out of little was far worse than spending a forlorn evening throwing more pots than she cared to throw.

Sarina, though, could not be placed neatly into the category of "old lover," a phrase Meg liked to spin off with nonchalance. Meg had allowed Sarina to enchant her—bewitch her, really—during long hours of seduction in which Sarina convinced Meg she was the only person who had ever lifted off the final layer of her protective sheathing. Mornings after nights with Meg were intolerable, Sarina had claimed; how could she build up the armament essential to the light of day? Later, when they lived together, Sarina still complained that the inward nature of their connection left her hobbled. Meg was bewildered as to why Sarina fled from the very intensity she had applied such tender calculation to evoke. The next thing Meg knew, of course, Sarina had asked to move on. Sheer love of perversity had pushed Meg to find out that that redoubtable final layer of sheathing was quite ready to be peeled back by the very next touch that came along. Once, during a wretched phone call months after their breakup, Sarina had offered in a spirit of the greatest goodwill, "If it hadn't been for you, I would've never been able to love anyone." For months Meg had marveled that Sarina meant those words as consolation. Now, years later, in this waiting room among fretting babies, Meg felt a sort of dull rage, a rage that she did not attempt to hold down.

She moved to the pay phone within sight of Kimble's seat. Just as she picked it up, not even pausing to plan what she would say to Sarina, a woman called her name.

Consuela Soto wore a gold-threaded shawl that immediately cheered Meg. Her lipstick was deep red, and although she was not smiling, she looked bemused. Meg could tell nothing beyond this. She gathered up the sleeping Kimble and followed Consuela.

In a moment, with Kimble asleep on her lap, she began plainly. "I wasn't consciously trying to elude the system, but I have to tell you what happened here."

Consuela listened to the story. Meg told her everything she knew about Shirley Marzola, and when she repeated what Honey had told her about Shirley's treatment of her daughter Anita, Consuela took up a pen and asked Meg to spell Shirley's last name. Listening to Meg enumerate her own qualifications as a potential foster parent, Consuela maintained a focused silence. She did not telegraph an opinion. When Meg was finished, she said, "You need a license. Where do you live?"

Meg told her.

"Do you have a bedroom for the child?"

"Well, you know, lofts. There's a section, in the back."

"OK. It's optimal to have a separate bedroom, but it's not essential if the guardian and the child are of the same sex. But is your place set up for a little girl? What experience have you had with child care?"

"We've managed so far," defended Meg. Suddenly Meg remembered that, on more than one occasion when she was younger, she and her feminist friends had devalued the station of motherhood, claiming any woman who could spread her legs could achieve it.

"We'll place the little girl tonight. It's protocol, and I'm sorry about it, but it has to be done. Then a few things will happen. We'll run Shirley Marzola through the system, and we'll send a caseworker out there. If we deem Mrs. Marzola unfit or if she chooses to relinquish custody, then we'll send someone out to you. We'll do an expedited home study. You might think the system is lucky to have you, Ms. Krantz, and I might think so, too, but you're going to have to sign an affidavit swearing you have no police record. Meanwhile, we file an Article 10 petition with family court. If the grandmother is out of the picture, they'll remand the child to us for placement. And if everything turns out, we'll release the little girl to you and grant you a temporary license. We'll give her a Title 19 card for medical. Then you can take it from there. Do you have any questions?"

"You're taking her? Now? I can afford her medical care."

Consuela shook her head. "You don't think nice-looking people turn out to be ax murderers?"

"If I were an ax murderer, why would I have brought her here?"

"True, but you did, and now we know this little girl exists. Forget the rules, honey, we have the news channels to answer to."

In the next moment, Consuela persuaded the groggy Kimble onto her own lap as Meg read over some papers, signed one, and tried not to look at Kimble, now justifiably her accuser. Deep in her thoughts, not daring to utter the slightest protest, Meg remembered her parents' words when one thing or another had spun out of control during Meg's long childhood: *This is insupportable; this cannot happen.* Meanwhile, composed in one another's company, Consuela and Kimble got up and walked together through the room and out an ugly brown door.

11

Meg could hear the sounds of Libby getting ready for their session. Elena had opened the door, nodded toward the upholstered bench in the vestibule, then swiftly disappeared. It was close to 10, and Libby was in her bedroom. Apparently she had just gotten up. Water ran from a faucet. In another moment there was a brief whoosh, and Meg could hear soft flapping sounds. From Libby came inarticulate mutterings. Then Meg heard a triumphant squawk and more pronounced whispers from Libby. A bird. It would be exotic. A toucan or a cockatoo. It had a name Meg could not quite make out, but a name of several syllables that Libby repeated. There were bangs and drawer slammings and indelicate throat clearings. Meg felt the absurdity of preparing to indulge her personal revelations while Libby advanced through the far more basic procedure of getting out of bed. She wanted to leave, yet she could not remember needing Libby so much as on this morning.

Finally, the door opened. Libby came out, blinking in the harsh light of her vestibule. She wore velvet leggings and a long sweater—it looked like angora and cashmere—and a string of pearls. Her pumps were black leather with an arc of wine-colored trim over the toes. But this was no perfect presentation: Clumps of hair stuck out chaotically, and Libby wore no lipstick. She smiled at Meg, delighted to see her as if she had just dropped by. She called to Elena to see if there was coffee, and she had to try several times before her voice carried. Her attempt at an impish smile did little to hide her embarrassment. Meg remarked on her cigarette smoking. Libby made a dismissive motion, then moved toward what Meg had come to think of as their room. It had never seemed so welcoming.

Sitting in the recliner, Meg found herself resenting the time she waited while Libby got coffee for both of them. When Libby was barely inside with the two steaming mugs, Meg burst out, "You've got to help me!"—a demand she had never made, a demand that sounded spoiled and histrionic to her own ears, and yet there was something in its expression she thoroughly enjoyed, as if release into patently bad behavior would liberate hidden energies.

"What *is* it, sweetie?" asked Libby. Her body craned forward. Her eyes, still swollen from sleep, widened in an effort to take Meg in. "What's happened?"

"They took Kimble! I brought her into Child Welfare because I had no choice, and they took her. I'm supposed to just twiddle my thumbs while the bureaucratic wheels turn, and then they're going to check me out. I don't know what I'm going to do; I don't know what's going to happen next."

"Of course you do," said Libby. "It's within your control."

"Libby! I'm going to see Sarina tonight. They took Kimble yesterday, and I'm going to see Sarina tonight, and I just was frozen this morning. Since when can't I be alone? You know I'm great at being alone. What's happening? And I've been remembering the weirdest episodes from childhood, like this time I accidentally pressed the shutter release on my father's Nikon and I thought the camera was going to explode. And then there was this thing with an egg baby I won't even get into. It's like getting LSD flashes, except I never dropped acid. I seriously don't know what's going on." Meg felt her vocabulary regress along with her splintered thoughts. She fell back and crossed her arms.

As if in mimicry, Libby sat back in her leather recliner. The tension drained from her face, and Meg saw her own hopes for a moment of prophesy vanish. Libby seemed suddenly disinterested, as if she put little stock in people slipping out of character, as if she knew it to be a quirk that would come to nothing.

"Libby?" asked Meg. "What are you thinking?"

Libby smiled. "Isn't that my line, darling?" She delivered this in a tone Meg had never heard, a tone lifted from a Noël Coward play.

Overlaid by a pervasive white glare, the anger took on pictures and shooting stars as in a cartoon, yet it was an implosion; Meg did not move. She saw herself hurling objects around the room, but she did not move a muscle. "Sometimes," she said coldly, "I think you are deliberately not helping me. Sometimes I think that nothing short of me walking in here and saying I shot my mother would get you on my side."

As Libby reached for a cigarette, she seemed to grow aware that something was amiss with her hair. Her free hand checked over her head, lighting on the ends of the misplaced tufts. Assessing the damage, her expression grew steely. "So," she said, "did you ask her for the dough?"

"No."

"Are you going to?"

"Probably not. For a lot of reasons. But one is that if I did, I think I'd be trapped in these childhood flashes forever."

Silence. Meanwhile, the column of ash at the end of

Libby's cigarette grew until it sloped toward her lap.

"Your ashes," said Meg.

Libby ignored her and let the ashes fall onto her sweater. She whisked them away. "What are you going to do next?"

"I don't know. I mean, I do know. I'm just getting my head in order today."

"You're wasting every minute we sit here. Every minute should be directed toward getting Kimble back." Libby paused. "Are you going to change her name to Krantz?"

"Excuse me?"

"When she's yours. When the adoption is final."

Meg looked at the Boston fern hanging by the window. A pleasant sight, it helped bring about a laziness, the sleepy comfort of this room. Her gaze grew faraway. Libby must have been watching her, because she called Meg's attention to the magazine picture in a gun-metal–gray frame near the door to the foyer. It was the only disagreeable sight in the room. It showed a hippopotamus standing, eyes half closed, in a pool of stagnant water. Libby had hung it there as a warning to her more ruminative customers.

Meg just shook her head. Throughout their months together she had often described a state in which contemplating the next possibility was so daunting that the room around her would shrink back and her vision would be reduced to a plane that encompassed no depth. When this phenomenon occurred Meg could not leave her loft. Yet in this state she was convinced that she possessed a gift for introspection that would repay her in bliss. In this state she would be happy to stare at a bowl of flowers from late afternoon until dark. Action and decision were anathema to this state, which she called The Magic Carpet. Libby was against the name. She had said that Meg was merely romanticizing a dysfunction so that she could cuddle up to it whenever the going got rough. She had said *she* would call The Magic Carpet by its real name: an attack of emotional paralysis. Over their months together she had pointed many times to the hippo standing in stagnant water.

"Meg, it's not true that I have deliberately not wanted to help you. But I'm not going to apologize for being tough. Do you remember when you first came to me and asked me all those fancy questions about my methodology? When I said 'I kick butt,' you and I both knew I was not going to get inducted into the psychoanalytic hall of fame. But you were willing to take a chance with me. And I was willing to take a chance with you. We have been committed to giving each other a chance ever since, and I, for one, think we have yielded some lasting results."

"Like what?" asked Meg.

"Like, for one, you have long since stopped trying to please me in the way you have tried to please your mother."

"That's because you accept me. My mother doesn't accept me for who I am."

"You're slipping, Meg. It's not the old dame's mission to accept you for who you are. It's her mission to milk you for everything you're worth. If you'd finally get that, then you'd be accepting her for who she is. This is a two-way street."

"But, Libby…"

"Yes? What? You still want her to understand you? It ain't gonna happen."

Meg looked at the Ansel Adams reproduction, then confronted Libby's face, puffy and startled-looking without make-up. "When I was over there the other day she told me about this time she went to St. Croix with my father. He said he'd go with her to get away from this woman he was having an affair with, but when they got there he had already put the woman up in a hotel. I didn't even know he'd had a mistress. My mother lived with that for years and never told me. I wanted to help her, Libby, and I felt paralyzed. Like him," she said, pointing to the hippo. "Are you telling me I shouldn't want to comfort her? Is that the key to freedom?"

Libby's expression grew serious. "That's horrible," she said. "I didn't know your father was that cruel." It was the first time she had expressed even a hint of solidarity with Charlotte. "What did you say to her?"

"Not a lot. I mean, I tried once or twice, but she was pretty resistant, and then I realized I was resistant. And now I feel so guilty, I can hardly stand it."

"Guilt leads to emotional paralysis," summed up Libby tidily. Again she gestured to the hippo. "He's got a history you wouldn't believe. Guilt and shame. Heartbroken, he couldn't get past being a lowly hippo. Look at him now."

"I'd like to emerge from here a little more than a lowly hippo," said Meg.

"I'd like you to emerge from here accepting we're all lowly hippos. There's elevation in acceptance."

"What're you today, Libby? The great Zen master?"

"There's elevation in acceptance," Libby repeated firmly.

"How can I help my mother? How can I help her yet make myself expendable to the process?"

"You can't. Concentrate on Kimble. Rarely does someone get an opportunity to be of such concrete help. You must rouse yourself." Libby leaned forward again. Her eyes were ringed in dark pigmentation that was usually concealed by makeup. Beyond this, her irises had a vapory look, maybe cataracts that Meg had never noticed.

"Someone like you," Libby continued, "has to consciously place herself in the flux of things. Some people gravitate toward the center of change, and some people find excuses to cower within the most quotidian existence. Every time you fear a change you have to ask yourself, *What's the worst that can happen?* In most cases, if you really put yourself in that worst-case scenario, if you really *put* yourself there as opposed to projecting during some dark, hippopotamus mood, you'll find the worst is within your ken. The older you get, the more you'll find you've already been there. Tell me I'm not right."

Meg did not appreciate being bullied into a response, yet she was relieved by Libby's words. She did not answer but nodded thoughtfully, aware she looked like the trusting supplicant.

"And now you need to know something." Libby leaned more forward still and reached out her hands. Without thinking Meg edged up on the couch and yielded her own hands. Libby looked down at her shoes, and when she tried to focus again on Meg's face, tears were in her eyes. "I'm afraid this will be our last session. I'm going into the hospital tomorrow. For surgery."

"Libby!"

"I'm not going to discuss it, sweetie—this is where my boundaries come in. Aren't I a hypocrite? I will tell you that I was going to give us time to prepare for, how should I say it, *adjourning* our sessions together, but I'm afraid I can't do that. What would you like me to do to make this easier for you?"

"You can't tell me anything?!"

"I'd rather not." Libby paused, then smiled wanly. "Did you know that for the last several months you've been my only customer?"

"It doesn't matter," Meg said immediately.

"I've *so* enjoyed you, Meg. You've brought me a great deal of pleasure, and I know you will bring pleasure to others too. None of us gives ourselves enough credit for just giving pleasure. You have more exploring to do. I won't say I cured you, but you wouldn't expect me to, would you?"

Meg was not listening. She was desperate to know what was wrong with Libby. As if she were still a volunteer at REACH, she wanted to know who was Libby's doctor, and if he or she was doing right by her, and what would happen to her when she was released from the hospital. "Who will take care of you?" she asked.

In the very next moment, Meg thought maybe Libby had a daughter who would now move in to care for her. Maybe Libby's own experience flew in the face of the advice she had always given Meg: Your mother can take care of herself.

"I will be taken care of" is all Libby said. "You shouldn't worry about me." Then she smiled. "Actually, you should worry. You just shouldn't wreck your life over it."

"What can I do for you?"

Libby released Meg's hands. "You can be my last success. This won't be hard for you. Just remember: If you sigh twice in a row, *rouse* yourself. The overexamined life is not worth living."

With that, Libby got up and reached out for Meg, pressed Meg's face into her angora shoulder, at once soft and prickly, and Meg just rested there, childishly refusing to participate in an embrace that was meant as good-bye. Then Libby broke away and jolted toward her bedroom, and Meg heard Elena rush to follow her, and she heard the unknown, exotic bird squawk a rowdy greeting before someone slammed the bedroom door shut.

∞   ∞   ∞

The sidewalk outside Libby's building on West 73rd Street shone with the mist of a recent drizzle. Still, a harsh radiance began to break through the clouds downtown. For weeks Meg had emerged from appointments with nothing but Kimble on her mind: picking her up or getting her fed, calming her down or shoring up her good humor, planning the next turn of their coexistence. Today, under the awful weight of Libby's announcement, when Meg left the building she felt a pull toward the absent Kimble, surely like an itch in a phantom limb. Meg could think of nothing to override the itch but to walk. Before Kimble, she had occasionally walked all the way from Libby's to Duane Street. She decided to make this walk today. At least her pace would distance her from the hippo in stagnant water.

Walking the streets of New York managed to both enliven and calm Meg. Endorphin high, she had heard. Maybe, but Meg preferred not to focus on the hormones. She did not look beyond the simple motion and its effects: a rising feeling of lightness the faster she went, a sweeping-out of all the turgid thoughts that led to immobility. Unlike Charlotte, who said walking for more than five minutes in New York was an assault on the senses, Meg perceived the crazy, bustling streets as the backdrop in one of those '30s New York scenes by Reginald Marsh or Raphael Soyer. The streets were the backdrop, and she was the central figure plugging her way ahead: a gal on the go, a woman with a destination.

Today she turned right on Broadway to walk down West End. She began to do what she frequently did when confront-ed by the urgent need to take some action: She imagined—no, actually, *entered*—other lives. Walking the streets of New York, she picked off her subjects in rapid succession—or they picked her, if they happened to round the corner at the right moment.

First came a woman about Meg's age who gripped a dark leather briefcase and wore a bright suit with large cloth buttons rimmed in gold and its own wide belt—the kind of outfit adver-tised in newspaper supplements. The woman looked tense and hurried. Meg decided she was a quota-driven insurance agent, a rookie, a convert from another profession that she had forsaken for the precise reasons she would renounce this one. She was on her way to an appointment, and when she passed by Meg could see her lips move. Perhaps she was rehearsing her sales pitch. Meg decided this woman would be owned by one soul-denying career after another. Her complaisance would one day lead to such monumental boredom, such an inalterable perception of life as an unending prairie, that she would methodically begin to store up barbiturates.

Just as Meg tired of the woman, whom she named Barb, just as she felt the surge of superiority that this game was meant to evoke, she passed a woman in such thorough possession of herself that by comparison Meg's constructed image of herself as a go-getter immediately faltered. What was the great advantage of going and getting when you could be this tall and serene woman carrying a bunch of anemones, your only mission to return to your airy upper-floor rooms and assemble the flowers in a ceramic jug by the window so that your visitor would see in a single glance both the flowers and the tops of the trees in Riverside Park? Why go anywhere and exert any ambition when you could be this woman, sitting with a close friend, listening and speaking until the vapor lifted off the Hudson and glints of pale sunlight appeared on the petals of the anemonies? This woman's name, Meg decided, was Imogene or Georgia, Eva or Millicent. She wanted to follow her home, to help her set out the anemones and meet her visitor.

Rather, Meg focused on the next passerby, a short, muscular man in leather regalia, a man whose flat, vaguely paternal expression cried out for Brooks Brothers. He was returning from a 3 A.M. date that had gone on much longer than planned; he had accidentally fallen asleep and had woken hours later,

alone in a strange room, disoriented and missing his own apartment. He looked dazed. The noon light turned the cruel intensity of leather chaps to pure folly. The man, who was not
young, looked in need of tender ministry. It was all Meg could
do not to stop him with a consoling pat, to let him know he had
an ally in her.

As in a Marsh or Soyer painting, every member of the
crowd was a type, a caricature who lent color to the big scene.
An appealing way to look at the world, a way that lulled Meg
immeasurably until she reached 59th Street and saw St. Luke's-
Roosevelt Hospital, where Barry Toffler had died. At that
moment she woke up to the coincidence of losses in her life—
Kimble and Libby within 24 hours—and she held up her right
arm to hail a cab.

∞   ∞   ∞

Home again, Meg looked about and saw everything that
was not homey about her loft. Two drywall partitions rose
three quarters of the way to the ceiling, leaving metal studs
exposed. There was not sufficient separation between Meg's
living area and her studio; she could see her kiln, electric
wheel, and drying racks from several vantage points in the loft.
A custom pine plank floor had been laid down in her living
area, but the floors of the rest of the loft were concrete, covered by sisal mats and rag rugs, mismatched in a way not
everyone would appreciate.

The kitchen was a source of pride because Meg had built
and painted its island cabinet, which she had fit with a slate
countertop. On Canal Street, she had bought a big double-basin
sink, constructed its housing, then hired Chris downstairs to do
the plumbing. For a lark Meg had ordered a refrigerator-freezer

in a designer color, Adobe Dust. It was a huge appliance with a crushed-ice machine and water fountain embedded in the freezer door, an appliance designed for a large suburban family. Meg did not usually put much in this refrigerator, but each time she opened one of its massive doors she became a solid citizen.

After years, the bathroom was still half done; she had purchased a claw-foot tub, whose height she had since regretted. There was no shower, and the sprayer attachment Meg had installed was awkward to use; she kept flipping it from hand to hand when she washed her hair.

Decoration was mainly in the form of pots: lopsided, unsellable goddesses from her recent collection, chipped platters, and several vases Meg had wired as lamps years before.

The way Meg lived had always suited her. She had, in fact, liked the integration of studio fixtures and furniture, had felt it somehow enhanced her seriousness as a potter. And the way she lived further separated Meg from Charlotte, whose Park Avenue interiors had been done by the firm of Moss & Leam, or "Mausoleum," as Meg called it to Libby. But today, out of the imagined eyes of a caseworker, Meg's loft was altogether lacking in whimsical appeal, a strictly utilitarian space too barren for a child without natural parents.

As Meg looked about, her determination regarding Kimble flagged once more. She thought of homes she knew with children in them. She had been to Juliet what's-her-name's once, before the divorce. Juliet had a two-and-a-half-year-old and a baby, and there was not a corner of their big house that was not altered in deference to these children. There had been a surfeit of gaudy-colored plastic things: vehicles to transport, contain, or benumb, as well as toys, electric-outlet sealers, nightlights, several expandable gates to block off stairs and doorways, and cheap-looking intercoms that carried and amplified colicky burbles to every room of the house. The books strewn about were not Kate Greenaway classics to be reverently perused in a rocking chair. There were thickly laminated board books whose close-up photos of beach balls and baby sneakers so overstated reality that Meg thought a truly dreamy child would recoil in offense. As Meg saw it, there was no room for interpretation in the life and environs of the modern baby, and she had been only too glad to leave Juliet's and head back to TriBeCa. She had the same, if more modified, feeling about city apartments that housed children. Meg had never thought about rearranging her personal space, a space that had hosted years of peaceful dreaming and solitude. Like a hidebound spinster from an inferior British novel, she suddenly felt the press of a fierce, unnatural regard for every little thing that was hers.

No, thought Meg as the phone rang, today she would force herself to be large and bountiful, to be Baroness Dripping In It, and she used the Baroness's husky, assured voice to answer the phone.

"Meg-leg?"

Amid street noise, the voice was faint.

"Yes? Kimble?"

Over the line came only the sound of a truck passing.

"Kimble! Is that you?"

"The lady said I could call. We're on an out-ting."

Kimble's by-rote use of the term *outing* took Meg's breath away. "Oh, sweetie! I miss you terribly. You know that you are only there *very* temporarily, don't you? You know what 'temporarily' means?" Meg realized she was wasting time and did not wait for an answer. "Now, where are you exactly?" She avoided asking who Kimble was with. She was not entirely sure what "emergency placement" meant, and she tried now to suppress her Gothic imaginings. She told herself that Kimble was with a loving, grandmotherly type whom the city prized, the kind of woman regularly extolled in church newsletters and on the feature pages of local newspapers.

"At the zoo. I saw Seal Island, and I told the lady I once saw it already, but Angel never saw it, and he told me to shut up or he was going to poke my eye out with his fingernail. He's got one really long fingernail and it's really ugly, and—"

"Kimble, listen to me. You just keep telling yourself it doesn't matter what things people say to you because you're going to be living with me very, very soon. Do you understand?"

Again, silence. Meg wondered how far Kimble was now from Seal Island, if she could see it, and if she remembered the day Barry had thrown back his head to yowl in time with the seal's bark, to charge the air with their unequal desires.

"How did you get my number?" asked Meg.

"From the woman Mrs. Soto. She gave it to me. Then this other lady who took us here, I forget her name, she let me press the buttons, 9-6-6…"

Meg wanted to ask Kimble what it was like for her in the moments after her departure yesterday. Again she restrained herself. This was her need, she decided, her need to see Kimble's misery as evidence of a mighty attachment. Her need, her ego. "Did the woman Mrs. Soto remember to give you your atomizer?" she asked. "Do you have it with you now?"

"Yes."

"Good, sweetie."

"What are you doing, Meg-leg?"

"Oh, I'm very busy. Getting ready for when you come back. You have to plan for what you want in life," she said. "And you have to keep concentrated on what you want. Can you do that?"

"I don't know what I want," said Kimble, for all the world like any adult Meg knew.

"No, I don't suppose you do," she said, and then they both said good-bye, and Meg went downstairs to get her van and drive to Macy's, where she picked out a child's bedroom set, a plastic playhouse, and several toys in hideous colors.

12

If Meg had felt herself turning into an observer of the passing crowd when she left Libby's, the transformation was complete by the time she approached Lotsa Pasta, where she was to meet Sarina. In preparation for their meeting Meg had put on Chanel No. 19, a silver bracelet from the Somerville Crafts Show, an opaque scarf with a shadowy design that looked like Sanskrit, and a new, dark shade of lipstick called Evenings Out. Even as she dressed she began to journey away from herself. Then on Eighth Avenue she meditated with undue focus on the name Lotsa Pasta. The owners were foolish, she thought. They should know that people did not go to Chelsea to stuff themselves. Maybe this would be her first comment when she saw Sarina. "Do you believe this name?" she would laugh wryly. No, too negative. What else could she comment upon? Could she be sardonic and upbeat at the same time, or was that stretching the limit?

Just before she reached the door of Lotsa Pasta, just before she began to fear some horribly witless remark would fall from her lips, there was a hand on her shoulder. Sarina was beaming in the way that Meg had once believed only she herself could inspire. In the next moment Sarina's arms were around her. Her embrace was close and mighty and full of meaning, of speechless reference to long-past events. Meg's return embrace was brisk and sure, the response of someone forsaken years before.

Inside Lotsa Pasta they were given a good corner table. The young man who shook out their fluted napkins was putting himself on display for the benefit of the two men at the next table. The final flourish was for them, although he glanced once at Meg and Sarina. "Do you believe this name?" asked Meg.

"It's pretty lame," said Sarina.

Could anyone who used the word *lame* in its recent incarnation possibly hold power over her? "How did your meeting with the Savory Sachet people go?"

"Speaking of lame names," said Sarina. "Fine. Good. They gave me a new line. It's called Potpourri For All Seasons. *Speaking* of awful names. Oh, look, we've been here all of two minutes, and we already have a theme."

This last, Sarina never would have said if she were not nervous herself. Meg looked at her. There was the slightest quiver about her mouth. Her wide, cockeyed mouth, a mouth Meg had thought of as mobile. Sarina's mouth had always betrayed emotions that her eyes refused to confirm. Meg had learned to watch her mouth during moments when she needed the truth. Now Sarina smiled, assurance returning. She looked wonderful. Thirty-five, two years younger than Meg. Her skin was as even and translucent as during their days together, yet the faint lines from the corners of her eyes so suited her that Meg wondered if she had attained her perfect age. She wore a rust-colored suede jacket over a black Danskin top. Deliberate, Meg knew—meant to show off her breastbones, the defining fallows that Meg had so often traced with her knuckle, then her nose (inhaling deeply), finally her tongue, her teeth. Meg turned her attention to the menu.

"So," said Sarina, "tell me what's happening with the little girl."

"Kimble," said Meg, momentarily disappointed that Sarina did not remember. After all, Meg had remembered "Savory Sachet." Small, deliberate recollections meant everything. "We're at a precarious point. I had to take her to Child Welfare yesterday to begin going through the ropes. Nothing's 100 percent until family court turns her over to me. And then I'll set up with an adoption lawyer."

"If you've decided to go through with this, I'm sure it will work out beautifully. You know, I always thought you would become a mother."

Meg did not know what to say. Sarina could not really believe that wanting something made it happen. Yet she had ended up with her house in the country.

"It has by no means been a black-and-white decision."

"I'm sure. But I've always thought it was something you needed," she added.

Meg just looked at Sarina. "Oh yes, a good anchor, in the absence of anything else."

"I didn't mean anything like that. What is she like?" Sarina leaned forward, rested her chin on her palm, gazed at Meg.

No one had ever asked Meg to describe Kimble. "She's an incredibly sweet little girl. I think that, all things considered, she's not acting as traumatized as you would expect. Of course, this is worrisome in some respects. She must have the most peculiar view of the world. First, her mother died, and her father stepped forward with his love. Then *he* died, and I came forward without missing a beat. We're like ducks at a shooting gallery: One gets picked off, and the next one advances." With this, Meg looked straight at Sarina. "That's not how it works out there. At least for most people."

"Of course not," Sarina readily answered.

"What I like best is how she talks to herself. The voice she uses when she talks to herself is so, I don't know, self-ministering. She could turn out to be fine, and that would be nothing short of a miracle. She has this doll her father gave her, Roller Queen, that she takes everywhere."

Sarina sat back. A deep breath filled her chest. The fallows deepened. She nodded slowly. "You're quite something," she said.

∞   ∞   ∞

In the beginning Meg was still a lens upon herself, herself and Sarina, transported to Meg's loft on the initiative of a single glance. Meg could not reliably judge if she were in danger. Yes, during the dinner she had confirmed what years ago she had sourly predicted: that Sarina's glibness, the ease with which she sought what she desired, would evolve into a shallowness that would undermine the grace and craft of her seductions. The older she got, Meg had predicted, the more vacant her flirtations would seem to any discerning woman. All during dinner Sarina had tossed off compliments. They never quite came off. Meg would not be the only one, she had reflected, to wonder at the accountability behind these compliments. There must have been half a dozen times during the evening that Meg had felt sure she had somehow ascended over Sarina—that since their time together she had regained a certain sense of expectation that Sarina would never know, a waiting posture that did not rely on flattery and calculated gestures. No, Meg had thought, this woman could no longer undo her. Yet there was the suede jacket and the Danskin top and how they were worn. There was the single glance that had propelled them here, and there was the fact that Meg had earlier made her bed just so and placed her newest goddess on the cherry-wood dresser across from it. There was all this and a measure of drunkenness and, worse, Sarina's fragrance, the one she had worn during the long nights of their first months together. In the end, Meg had to stop assessing the danger, had to discard the lens, had to stand in unbearable anticipation as Sarina slid the opaque scarf onto her own neck and then back over Meg's, driving an endless loop, an outer friction that made something uncoil steadily within her. Finally, it was Meg who grabbed hold of both scarf ends and drew Sarina so close that a tiny gasp escaped her, one gasp that slapped something hard as a blow over the tentative stirrings Meg had tried to hold down.

For the next two days the loft became the undisputed house of her adulthood. Somewhere in the middle of the first night Meg rolled up Kimble's futon and stashed it in a closet. Kimble's furniture had not yet been delivered from Macy's, and Meg had not had time to bring up the toys before she had gone to meet Sarina at Lotsa Pasta. The toys were still in the back of the van in her parking garage on Hudson.

Over her two days with Sarina, Meg's attention fell only on those of her belongings she had failed to notice recently: books on art and mythology and ancient pottery she had bought in the days she had lived with Sarina, gorgeous minerals tucked away on bookshelves, a row of framed prints of women by Rodin that she had hung across from the claw-foot tub but had not studied much in recent years.

Sarina had always spent a good deal of time simply look-ing. Sometimes she would nod in approval of a particular sight, as if her very appreciation had brought it into being.

Meg imagined this looking, this appreciative looking, was a great part of her experience on Leah's acres. Meg found she was jealous not of their life together but of how Sarina permitted looking to be its own worthy purpose. In the claw-foot tub before the Rodin prints, in bed gazing at the white enamel ceiling fan, noticing as if for the first time the pleasing slant of its tapered blades, Meg felt the danger and the paradox once more: If Sarina was untrustworthy—relentlessly casual—then how could simply lying beside her, staring at a ceiling fan, fill Meg with such happiness?

This question became critical during their second night together, when Sarina excused herself to go not far enough away to call home. Her side of the conversation was stunningly convincing. She told Leah that the Savory Sachet people had been so pleased with her proposed packaging that they had immediately put her on a plane to Baltimore, where she showed her work to the art director at their home office. There had not been a moment to call. She was back in New York now but too exhausted to head home tonight. She would call her tomorrow to tell her which plane she'd be on. When Sarina lowered her voice to whisper her good-byes, when her tone tripped for a moment over passion on its way to cooing, Meg understood that Leah did not question her story for a moment.

Sarina returned to the bedroom, still wearing nothing. Meg freed herself from the tangle of smooth sheets and sat up straight. "Tell me, did Leah drop out of Hunter when she discovered her appalling lack of intuition?"

Sarina had the good grace to flush slightly, but she did not hesitate to return to bed and smooth back Meg's hair. "That might have sounded easy to you, but it was extremely difficult. I haven't been with anyone but Leah since you. And now you again."

For a moment Meg was startled into silence. Then she answered, "What if I believed you? What if I asked you to consider that remark might carry something in the way of consequences? Would you be willing to suffer some upheaval?"

"Oh," said Sarina, now rearing back some. "Passion and consequences. I forgot that about you. Your stubborn twist on crime and punishment."

"Well, don't. Once is enough."

"You've always been too civilized for me, Meg." There was little question that "civilized" was an insult.

"You just lied to Leah because you're living in an arrangement that carries consequences. Your very lying is proof you can't evade a certain kind of behavior. It's entrenched in the way you chose to live, the most important decision you made. You're 35, Sarina. Somehow you got to be that age. This free-spirit thing is getting old."

At this, Sarina got up and put on her jeans. She reached for Meg's Sanskrit scarf and threw it over her shoulders so its ends covered her breasts. It was so like Sarina to choose an article of clothing that belonged to Meg in order to retreat from Meg.

"Look around you, honey," said Sarina. "This loft is so you when you were in your twenties. The unfinished bathroom is *your* refusal to grow up. The refrigerator is your way of thumbing your nose at anyone who expects more of you—probably still at Charlotte. I may have my shortcomings, and you may have suffered particularly for them, but I wouldn't settle for this provisional way of living. That's why I left New York."

Quietly Meg added, "That's why you found yourself an heiress. Let's remember *how* you got to Vermont. My suburban refrigerator might be a little kitschy, but at least it doesn't place me in a chapter from a trashy novel."

Sarina looked like she was about to say something, then

just exhaled loudly, her fine posture collapsing along with the release of her breath. Lack of sleep showed in her eyes. Her brow was no longer smooth.

Meg knew what she had said was untrue. She believed that no one lived in trashy novels, that trashy novels were simply written by and for people who were not in the mood to delineate themselves. She knew that everyone who experienced a moment's solitude in a day or in a lifetime took themselves seriously.

Although Sarina fingered the hem of Meg's scarf and did not look up, she projected her words in a voice husky and modulated, a terrible draw to anyone who might be attracted to her. "So you don't want to think more about us, to give us some more thought?"

Meg straightened herself up on her elbow, which trembled from the unaccustomed burden of her weight. There was a sudden inability to respond, at which time she had the sly dawning: *I can say, "No, I don't want to think more about us," and then think about us as much as I please.*

"You don't particularly care about being a mother, remember?" Meg said.

"But I don't know that for certain," said Sarina. "I can be flexible."

"Yes," Meg acknowledged. "You can be flexible."

When Meg got up from bed, she saw from her outside glance that Sarina had not recovered her neat posture and that beneath the hem of her jeans, the angularity of her ankle bone—a shape that had always seemed oddly personal to Meg, an exact curve she once felt sure was designed especially for her—was now just someone's anklebone. Meg put on a sweater and went to her closet to look for what else to wear.

All those toys were still in the back of her van, and Meg had a rush of panic that they had been there too long, that if they had not been stolen, they might actually wither from neglect, as if orphans themselves.

13

Two days later, as she descended the manual elevator to let in the caseworker from Child Welfare, Meg was still thinking about Sarina. It was curious that she had dedicated every thought to Sarina—dedicated and narrated, despite the oppressive melancholy that had surrounded their parting. As she pushed open the heavy outside door, it struck Meg that over the years she had fallen into silently addressing many of her actions to someone whose capacity to nurture was like that of an ordinary high school cheerleader, one who rallied only around triumph. This realization was not new, was in fact old, but now it slipped from the cerebral to the visceral, to the site of Meg's body that collected shames both small and large, the site which had a back flow that could drag her from the brink of sleep into a week of insomnia. Now she had to immediately usher in a new and plausible beginning.

"Mrs. Cheney? Welcome. I'm Meg Krantz!" she declared, smiling.

"Yes. How do you do? I'm Mrs. Cheney from CWA." The woman let out a small giggle, as if she needed to confirm her identity to herself. She was a white woman about ten years older than Meg, whose wiry, chin-length hair fanned out from her face in a brown-and-white blur. She carried a beat-up briefcase and a muslin recyclable bag with vegetables in it. Meg had the same recyclable bag with a globe printed on the front, and she was grateful, thrilled even, that she had hung it from the kitchen hook that had previously held her purse-size mace.

"Consuela told me you're known for your incredible punctuality." As confirmation she held her watch before the woman's eyes. Then she worried that this would be perceived as too buoyant, too condescending. "Thank you for coming," she added, sounding as robotic as Charlotte at her annual New Year's party.

Meg had accomplished a great deal over the past two days. She and Chris downstairs had erected a fireproof stall around her kiln with a door that could be locked. She had cleaned thoroughly. An unsuccessful effort to purge Sarina from her thoughts had at least resulted in great orderliness, and now Meg felt uplifted as she stepped into her loft.

"Oh," said Mrs. Cheney, her tone polite and remarkably neutral.

"I have tea, coffee, Snapple. Let's see, what else? There's some pineapple juice. Kimble loves—"

"No, thank you. I hope you won't mind showing me around a bit." Mrs. Cheney walked into the studio, stood before the drying rack. "This is your pottery?"

"Yes." Meg thought it best to add nothing, but found it disquieting that her pottery was being looked over as a commodity, even though it was exactly that.

"Have you had a fire inspector here? Is this loft legal?"

"I have a Certificate of Occupancy," said Meg. She did not add that she had secured it only months before, after she and the other tenants had brought the building up to code. "Would you like to see it?"

Mrs. Cheney smiled. "Others would, believe me." She looked at the housing around the kiln. "What's this?"

Meg unlocked the new door and showed Mrs. Cheney her kiln. She explained about the fireproofing, implying that she was so safety-conscious the stall had always been there.

"Now, this child you're interested in adopting—Kimble Toffler. You understand that she is under the care of the commissioner of Social Services. All of that has been explained to you?"

"Yes."

"And did they tell you what we'll need from you? This includes your birth certificate or a marriage license. You probably don't have pay stubs, so your tax returns will do. You don't have employer references either, do you?"

"I have several buyers I've worked with for years. What else?"

"Let me see," said Mrs. Cheney. She put on a pair of half-glasses, the kind that can be selected from a drugstore rack, and took some papers from her bag. "I have here an affidavit for your signature. Feel free to read it. We need you to swear you've never been convicted of a felony." She gave Meg a rueful smile, the bureaucrat going by the book. "Other states are tougher, believe me. They print prospective foster parents and run a police check on them."

Meg scanned the affidavit and signed it. "I can get you my birth certificate or a copy. I have tax returns going back forever. Would you like to see Kimble's bedroom?"

Mrs. Cheney followed Meg to the back of the loft, where Meg had constructed an extra wall around Kimble's sleeping area. There was no furniture, but Meg had unpacked her other purchases from Macy's, including a postmodern play tower consisting of steel-gray plastic cubes that fit together at odd angles.

"That's a little…well, I guess it makes a statement."

"I haven't quite hit the motif," apologized Meg. She showed Mrs. Cheney a picture of Kimble's bedroom set on order from Macy's.

Mrs. Cheney nodded absently. Meg knew she sounded thoroughly absurd. Though Mrs. Cheney might not love the minimal look of the playhouse, what serious person—surely what emissary of the commissioner of Social Services—gave a rat's ass about a vanity with a Broadway stage mirror? Like the drag queen who years before had done needlepoint at REACH's front desk, Meg had created a parody of the straight woman, in this case a mother whose greatest stock is her daughter's creamy complexion. Next she would be telling Mrs. Cheney she had ordered mother and daughter bonnets from the Spiegel catalog.

"Of course, she might not take to the vanity," explained Meg. "She might use it as a second desk or something. That's up to her. Would you like to sit down up front?"

Meg led Mrs. Cheney to her old couch, covered by afghans and throws. Once seated, Mrs. Cheney set right in. "I need to ask you what kind of child-rearing experience you've had, Miss Krantz. I know you touched on this with Consuela Soto, but it's not an inconsiderable part of our evaluation. Especially in the case of single women, who may have no extra resources for child care, we need to know what preparation they have. And we need to know who else will be in the child's life—relatives, boyfriends, special friends…"

"I'm glad you brought that up," said Meg. "You should know that I'm a lesbian. I'm not with anyone right now, but, of course, that could change." Although Meg had planned this announcement knowing full well the city could not discriminate, it was stated with an outward breeziness that belied downright terror, a fear that made the liberty-ship door vibrate in the foreground of her vision, a nervousness that had not abated over so many similar moments throughout the years. She plowed beyond. "I don't have a large family, but my mother lives on Park Avenue, and we speak a couple of times a week. She knows Kimble, and she supports this plan."

"Uh-huh," said Mrs. Cheney. "We have some gay parents in the foster system. Some of them go on to adopt. But what exactly *is* your child care experience?"

"Oh, I have an extremely close friend, an old roommate, actually, who lives in Delaware, and I'm godmother to her little boy. She has an older daughter too. From the time they were very young they've both stayed with me in the city."

"I mean long-term experience?"

A lie that might have cost something, that could be checked out, and it wasn't good enough. Meg added weakly, "Well, they're teenagers now, so there's been consistency throughout the years."

Mrs. Cheney wrote something down. When she looked up again, Meg feared it was to get Cami Porter's name. Not only was her story not verifiable beyond Cami's corroboration, but why should Cami, who would never be Cami Toosdaneldanewspickle Porter, have any reason to lie for Meg?

"Now, I see that Kimble has asthma. What sort of experience do you have in managing asthma?"

"Her asthma was diagnosed when she was with me. I got her to a hospital and got some good training from the staff there." Meg heard her voice as clipped and withheld. How many natural parents could answer these questions satisfactorily?

"Miss Krantz, I must tell you honestly that as a single, self-employed woman you may not be regarded as the ideal candidate in this case. This is not my subjective judgment; it is reality."

"Kimble and I have a close, established relationship. I took care of her when no one else was there. Doesn't that count for something?"

"It counts for a great deal. But I have to be candid. Two-parent homes are still favored. And I have to also remind you that this is affected by the fact that Kimble falls into the highly coveted group of children who are healthy and mentally able." Mrs. Cheney uncrossed her legs, leaned forward, fingered an incense holder Meg had made years before. "We have an overwhelming number of HIV children in the system," she added. She began to reach into her briefcase, to withdraw a book whose spine Meg recognized from her visit to the Child Welfare Administration. It was a blue book of available children, a document so brazen in its purpose that Meg involuntarily averted her eyes. She put a hand on Mrs. Cheney's arm.

"Did I complete all the paperwork with Mrs. Soto, or do you have more?" Meg's voice was steely. There was no doubt that the woman was telling her she qualified nicely to care for an HIV-positive child, but her credentials were dubious when it came to a healthy one. "I appreciate what you are telling me, but I spent eight years holding the hands of dying people, and I think it is my right to try to adopt a healthy child. I know it's my right."

There was little more discussion, and Meg was careful to line up the elevator precisely with the lobby floor before she led Mrs. Cheney to the front door. As she went back upstairs, she felt her moment of assertion grow palpable; it buzzed inside her wrists, behind her ears, a dull accompaniment to her vision of one child lingering day after night and then dying between sheets that did not offer up Tinkerbell or the Little Mermaid, coarse sheets that offered uninterrupted whiteness.

∞   ∞   ∞

Meg had promised herself she would rise at 7:30 the next morning and set to work on an order for New England Arts, a retail store in New Hampshire that looked like an old-time crafts guild. At 9:30 she was still in bed staring at the blades of her ceiling fan. From outside, she heard the harsh squeal of truck brakes, the erratic drill of a jackhammer, the calls of construction workers, the whoosh of Hudson Street traffic.

A 37-year-old woman alone in a bed amid the world's bustle, a hippo in stagnant water. She sat up and massaged her neck, walked over to start coffee. She could call Libby, she thought. She could leave a message on the machine. She might use the phrase "I'm just checking in to see how everything went." Out of decency someone would call her back. Elena or the phantom daughter. This is what she would do, Meg decided, after she had had her coffee. Then her own phone rang, and Meg watched the light on the answering machine beside it blink as a voice said, "Meg, this is Ray. From REACH. I wanted to—"

"Ray!"

"Hi. Listen, hon, I haven't gone into work yet, but I wanted you to know off the record that I got a call from Shirley Marzola yesterday. She doesn't really know what the pediatric department does; she thinks we're a group-care setting. She wanted to know if Kimble was with us. I won't go into the details, but I need to tell you that she thought Kimble was positive and now she knows she's negative. That's all I can say. I just wanted you to know."

Meg glanced desperately over to the coffeemaker, a third of the way through its brew. She snatched away the pot and threw a sponge over the burner to soak up the drips while she poured coffee into her waiting mug. She closed her eyes, took a sip. "Does she know where Kimble is now?"

"I didn't give her Consuela's name, if that's what you mean. I told her Kimble came to the playroom during Barry's illness and shortly after his death, but she's not a client any longer. That's the truth, right? You're no longer a volunteer, she's no longer a client. Look, I'm sorry about what happened. We've both screwed up here."

"It's not good news. But thank you. Really. You've been a great help all along."

Ray coughed into the phone. "Sorry. Thanks."

"You OK?"

"Oh, yeah, fine. Just a touch of TB, PCP, and general pulmonary dysfunction. Just a lesion or two on the old lungs."

Alarmingly, Meg had no idea if Ray was kidding. "You going in today?" she asked helplessly.

"Yeah."

"Good!" she declared in her halest voice, a voice that emerged from her first year of volunteering, a robust and ugly voice.

∞   ∞   ∞

"Party, please?" This was the same doorman who months before had attended to only his racing forms as Meg and Kimble breezed through the Rego Park lobby. At first Meg didn't follow. Party?

"Oh! Shirley Marzola. What is it, 8G?" Meg hadn't called ahead. "Tell her it's Meg Krantz."

Meg heard some static over the doorman's intercom; she thought she heard an epithet or at least a tone that contained one. The doorman's expression was impassive. "8E," he said, and waved her up.

Shirley was posed in the dim light over her door frame and offered no greeting as Meg walked off the elevator. She wore a blue cotton housedress whose stiff, scalloped piping looked as though it would leave thorny scratches along her neck as she moved, as she marked up *her* racing forms. She looked Meg up and down. "A person has to be pretty low," she said.

Meg's heartbeat quickened; she felt her throat heat up. In her world, accusations had always been heavily cloaked, had slipped in through the back door.

"I can't say I'm particularly proud," she said.

"*Proud*? A sacrilege. A terrible thing. What kind of a person? And you, a volunteer, a *buddy*, this is what a buddy does? There's terrible trouble in the world, and you give an innocent little girl the AIDS!"

Meg winced. This woman, she thought, this woman who gambles in Atlantic City and carouses in Palm Beach now comes forward, wounded, with a bulletin: Terrible Trouble in the World.

"May I come in, Shirley?"

"The hall's good enough."

Meg grew panicked. Certain conversations required certain poses—a crossed leg for earnest probing, hands in the pockets for confrontations. She had no chair, no pockets. The opposite wall was miles away. She stood there marooned in the middle of a hall that smelled of boiled cabbage. Across from her was Shirley Marzola, no makeup, exposed upper arms that were pockets of loose flesh, the glint of a gold charm around a swollen ankle—Charlotte overturned, Charlotte in the dappled mirrors of Rego Park.

Meg crossed her forearms, perceived the aggressiveness, let her arms dangle foolishly. "Why do you want her?"

"She's my granddaughter."

"What about Sal Zito? He doesn't want children."

"Sal's gone. Let me give you a life lesson. Never trust a professional pallbearer."

"But you had your own uncertainty about Kimble. Barry told me. You indicated as much yourself."

"Do I owe you an explanation? She's my granddaughter. She's my Anita's baby. I want her because she's mine."

Meg was quiet for a moment. "Mrs. Marzola, there's a new gap in your life. To my way of thinking, that's what this is about."

"So? All our lives are gaps. We try to fill them. Anita tried with God. I go to my Atlantic City. You think you have no gaps, you who wants a stranger's child?"

A door opened at the end of the hall, and a man came out with a garbage bag. He did not acknowledge Shirley and Meg but seemed to regard their hallway intimacy as an extension of his territory. A popular piano tune followed him into the hallway. He took his garbage to the incinerator.

"A player piano," Shirley told Meg, her face relaxing as she delivered the intimate news. "He can't play a note. Hello, Mr. Holland."

The man looked up and waved, more in dismissal than in greeting. An inveterate misogynist, thought Meg.

"I do want a stranger's child, I admit this. I never thought about wanting a child, never in a serious way, until Kimble and I were together during her father's death. We were sitting out in the hall of St. Luke's playing Go Fish. She was being awful that day, but I had this very odd experience of backing up and seeing the two of us as if we were in a painting. Did you ever look at two people together in a painting, or even framed by the TV screen, and they are just two people in a moment of time—but there is something so rock-hard and permanent about the two of them that you feel comforted just looking? My feeling about my own presence changed that day. It was less elated, less buoyed up by this great sense of possibility that I have known, but I felt bound to a picture, a scene, the two of us. Barry would die in that room, and I would fill his role. Whatever Barry did in his life, he wanted to repent with Kimble. Maybe he couldn't have, even healthy, but there is this terrible chaos in Kimble's universe now. Somebody has to make it right for her. Somebody has to give her gravity."

"And you think that's you? You think you're entitled?"

"I have the advantage of being no one to her. I'm neutral. I can stop the damage."

"You come here, stand in my hall, and tell me I am the damage."

Meg shook her head. She shifted her weight onto her left leg. "No, I'm reminding you you'll be well into your seventies when Kimble's ten."

"I know you're not so young either."

Meg smiled.

"I still have some Atlantic City money," said Shirley. "I'll get us a one-bedroom."

"Mrs. Marzola...the Child Welfare Administration has you on record. You must know this." In point of fact, Meg was not sure this was true.

Now Shirley opened her door wider, beckoned Meg inside. She did not offer her a seat. They stood in the tiny vestibule,

Meg beneath a ceramic fixture from which dangled a birthday card: an old woman straddling a Harley-Davidson.

"I won't tell you all the insanity. Anita, my daughter, was a true demon. The drug speed at age ten. Let *me* explain about two people in a picture. When I was raising Anita alone I was trapped in a picture. She did nothing but try to get out of the picture, and believe me, I'd be better off without her in it, but I had my duty. I looked at her and thought she should be out in the world, *I* need the protection here. She drove my car when I was at work—this is age 12. There was a crash, juvenile court; it was me who got dressed down by the judge. She had this mission to go out there and conquer, and I was the feeble one, the one who needed her feet rubbed after work and who sniveled she couldn't make it, the world was too mean, the bosses too hard, the bills too much, a waterfall that never stops. So now and then I left. And usually stayed away too long, which is why a total stranger like you knows about me and Child Welfare. The convent was how Anita punished me. She put herself in a place that housed her opposite. A joke. What worse way for a child to punish her mother than by turning her own life into a joke?"

Meg nodded. Thirty-seven, and still she identified with the adolescent Anita in this story. What power did Meg ever hold over Charlotte but to turn herself into the opposite of Charlotte's ideal?

"So the demon becomes Little Miss Muffet, and then the scene changes again and she meets this con man, and she can't make up her mind if she's Little Miss Muffet or her old demon self. Then she gets the AIDS and dies. So that's the story: I had a daughter, I did a lousy job, now I don't have a daughter."

"Where was Anita's father?"

"Married, like the rest of them. Don't you know about

conservation-minded women like me? We only use recycled."
Shirley backed up a couple of steps. "So now you're in my
house. I have some Sara Lee. The little coffee rolls."

Meg nodded slowly, as if she were considering a particularly tricky point of negotiation. "OK. That would be nice."

Shirley, too, nodded slowly. She turned toward the kitchenette, which abutted the vestibule. Meg watched. Shirley
wore satin slippers with two-headed dragons on the toes. A
rubber sole momentarily clung to something sticky on the
linoleum floor. A thick blue vein rose to the surface of Shirley's
tensed calf. The back of her neck and top of her shoulders were
obscured by rolls of flesh. Her skin was at a decided remove
from her skeleton, the center of energy, youth itself. Skin with-
ers from the bone or swells too far beyond it. One or the other.

Shirley set four tiny frozen rolls onto an uncovered grill
inside a toaster oven. She bent her head to fiddle with the knob
that controlled the temperature. Meg saw a star burst of pure
white beneath the limp, reddish dye. "These will defrost, then
heat up," Shirley explained. She set milky glass plates on laminated place mats. "My life has come to nothing," she said.

A neighbor ran a faucet. The moment intended for Meg's
contradiction slipped by.

"But I have enjoyed many things," she quickly added.
"Some people think pleasure *is* purpose. I have had pleasure."

Meg did not want to hear about Shirley's pleasure. She had,
in fact, an unreasonable certainty Shirley was about to divulge
some particular aspect of her orgasmic history. "I'm sure you
have," she said briskly. "You know, if you were to call the Child
Welfare office, particularly Mrs. Soto or Mrs. Cheney there, if
you were to call them and recommend me, it might make all
the difference for Kimble."

As Meg took her place at the table, Shirley turned her back, extended her arm toward the toaster-oven door, and asked, "And why should I do such a thing?"

"No reason, really. I'm not telling you I deserve your favor; I don't. This would be practical."

"And why practical?"

"Because if all you do is call to recommend me, you won't be under scrutiny yourself." Again, Meg had no idea if this were true. Consuela Soto might well have already checked out Shirley.

"You become just a family member who's not able to take Kimble on," continued Meg. "And because, frankly, I'm border-line for them. You could make a real difference. And because you need me."

"So, like you, now I need a stranger."

"I will make it my business to see that Kimble stays a part of your life."

"And I should believe a person who says a little girl has the AIDS as casual as she has a sniffle?"

"Yes."

"I ask a liar if I can believe her, and she tells me yes; I lis-ten," summed up Shirley Marzola. She sighed, waved her hand over a steaming coffee roll, bit into it.

Meg started to eat too. The chemical sweetness became part of the moment, leaving her delirious, imbuing the apart-ment's cheap trinkets, hideous on any other day, with a modest beauty. This morning a stuffed pair of dice displayed inside the hutch possessed a soul.

14

For the past month, these suggestions of winter: at night a sudden, frigid wind blasting up Duane Street; a gray afternoon sky that clung to building tops; unexpected sputterings from the loft's ancient risers. Meg had wrapped these risers in thick insulation. They looked like giant silver casts. She had done this before Mrs. Cheney's visit, during a week of erratic weather. Today winter had arrived. Snow flurries whirled about hysterically. People surrendered to unflattering hats. They set their expressions for months of forbearance. Meg, though, did not wear a hat. As she entered the Snowy Egret, a new restaurant in the East Sixties, she unwrapped from her neck a length of hand-woven chenille, a gift from Cami, and approached Charlotte, already seated by a small fire, her fingers worrying the stem of a wine glass.

Charlotte eyed Meg's new leather bomber jacket. "Oh, dear. Another winter without proper attire."

" 'Hello, Meg, it's nice to see you,' " said Meg flatly.

"All right," said Charlotte. "I'm sorry. There, I started with an apology."

The waiter appeared. Before he could say anything Charlotte asked, "A drink to start?"

"The house red, thank you," said Meg.

"I have an order for you!" sang Charlotte—too loud, her voice carrying over the sound of the wood fire to the next table. "From Juliet Tree. She's back to using 'Tree' now. All kinds of changes are going on for her. She's been taking a course on ancient mythology, and she's *fascinated* that you sculpt goddesses."

"Throw," corrected Meg.

"Besides her interest in mythology," said Charlotte, leaning closer, "she's trying to get pregnant and finding it's not quite as easy as it used to be."

Meg wondered if she could ignore the obvious bait, then dismissed the idea as impossible. "She's found someone already?"

Charlotte, flushed and healthy-looking, leaned closer still. "The husband's lawyer! The slick one who robbed her of the White Plains house!"

"Oh, shit," said Meg. "Unbelievable. I thought maybe divorce would be an opportunity for her."

"What kind of opportunity?" Charlotte had a tendency to put on a Betty Boop-style dim-wittedness. It was meant to curtail any feminist-sounding remark from further evolution. "Life is a highly complicated affair, Meg."

As the waiter set down Meg's wine, Charlotte took a sip of hers. "Passion can lead people up unpredictable paths," she explained.

"What kind of pot does she want?" asked Meg.

Deflect, Libby had advised. When Charlotte spoke from the mountaintop about passion, clearly the province of heterosexuals, when she uttered pronouncements on the nature of adult love as if Meg were merely a rapt spectator, simply deflect. "Talk about the weather, for Christ's sake!" Libby had instructed. And she had nodded vigorously, in complete accord with Meg's outrage over Charlotte's mannered superiority. She had not, like other therapists Meg had interviewed, told Meg to be patient. "Talk about the weather and how life is not the same without B. Altman's and whatever else you don't give a fuck about," Libby had said. "I don't believe in trying to change people. I don't believe in making nice in order to get them to see your side. I believe in toughening up."

"Which goddess does she want? What size? She'll have to wait six weeks. I'm getting my Christmas shipments together."

"Six weeks? She could get pregnant in six weeks!"

"Good. I hope she does."

"Why don't you get more studio help, honey? I would be happy to advance you the first month's salary. The added productivity would repay me easily. I'm not worried."

"I might get someone eventually," said Meg vaguely. She picked up the menu. It seemed unfathomably delicate in her hands: a buff parchment with ornate script, the name of each dish spaced as carefully as its actual incarnation would be on a plate. Medallions of lamb. Meg was hungry. She was tired. Medallions of lamb would revive her. It was expensive. She would have it.

The waiter came, and Meg watched as Charlotte ordered from him. Like many waiters at Upper East Side restaurants, he was masterful at alternately revealing and masking his sexuality. Tremendously attentive, he described particular dishes with a studied, almost brooding care to their sensual appeal, down to the secondary aroma of a particular sauce. He looked directly into Charlotte's eyes as he answered her questions. In one moment he pushed his square jaw forward and his mouth appeared brutish; in the next he lowered his lids with their uncommonly long lashes. Yes, if these women were asked, they would have to say that their waiters probably liked men, but they were so handsome that in the world at large it hardly seemed to matter. Meg watched as Charlotte gave him her order, in the end just a grilled tuna, and she saw that Charlotte was genuinely flustered, that she wanted to please the waiter, that he meant something. In that moment Meg saw that one day people who had previously meant nothing to Charlotte, who had been one of a thousand ornaments during the day, would gain definition, would acquire a place in her world; she would conjure them before bed or during a walk the next day. Charlotte was lonely, and as always when Meg recognized this, she longed, in equal measure, to hold her and to run headlong into her own life.

The waiter now turned for Meg's order, and he understood instantly that she was a different story. In a single look they acknowledged every nuance of the moment. He took in the leather jacket draped over the chair and knew that Charlotte was far from sanguine about her daughter's life. He knew that Meg was not impressed with his talent for coddling women of means. He knew, too, that she regarded his seductive manner as a self-betrayal and probably despised him on principal. Yet this was decidedly his turf. He nodded approvingly at her selection of the lamb medallions and left. In this Upper East Side neighborhood, Meg knew, those who should be natural allies never are.

"So," said Meg, nervous suddenly at the prospect of silence, "how are you? Are you planning any new trips?"

"Ida and I are talking about later this winter. We're thinking of Estoril or Majorca. There are some other women who will probably join us." She paused only briefly. "Did you ever stop to think that widowhood is a culture of sorts? I don't know what the demographics are, but I know we're underrepresented on Madison Avenue. Even Hal Lasser—you remember him, he and Madeline retired to their place in Bermuda last year—he used to be at Doyle Birnbach, *he* says we're underrepresented. He says the advertising industry knows it, but they don't want to include us because it's commonly known that we're depressing. He said the advertisers just bank on us buying the products aimed at younger people. And of course we do, which is why no one knows we're a culture."

Meg just looked at her mother. She did not know exactly what to say. Charlotte was right, of course, but even Meg counted on her mother's silence about the basic injustice of her social invisibility. After all, she had no wish to enter into solidarity with Charlotte on the matter of being marginalized.

"If being perceived as insignificant keeps you out of the advertisers' board rooms, you should consider yourself lucky."

"Meg, you can dismiss advertisers all you like, but everyone knows they just reflect what people are thinking."

A woman came to their table and showed them a basket of steaming popovers. A gingham napkin lined the basket, giving it a country feel, like Kimble's Amish pinafore folded in Meg's bureau in the loft.

"Oh, how lovely!" declared Charlotte, her customary way of accepting something offered.

Meg also accepted a popover, opened it, and let its steam escape and vanish before she said, "I don't need money to hire an assistant right now, but I could use a loan to take some time off. Just a month or two. I'm getting custody of Kimble. If all the paperwork goes through, I'll have her in a day or two. I think I should devote the first few weeks to setting her up, getting her in nursery school, thinking some things through. I could use the time. I'm going to start trying to adopt right away."

Charlotte chewed slowly, then laid the remainder of her popover down. She fingered a tiny pair of silver tongs, absently picked up a cube of raw brown sugar, dropped the cube on the tablecloth, retrieved it again with the tongs. "Most of my money is tied up," she said. "Locked into notes of one kind or another. It's not as easy for me to create cash as you might think."

"OK."

Their dishes came. Meg saw the garnishes first: a new kind of parsley, a slender bunch of champagne grapes springing off the plate.

Charlotte did not begin eating. She looked for their waiter, the man for whom she might come to this restaurant again. "I'm terribly sorry, but might I try your endive salad? I meant to order it before, and then it entirely skipped my mind." Her voice was thick, over-resonant.

"Of course. Would you like it now or later?"

"Oh, now, I think. Meg?"

"No. Thank you."

The waiter and Meg did not look at each other. Charlotte waited for her salad to arrive. Meg, too, sat and waited. She took some water. When she looked up, she saw Charlotte's face was drained of color, her jaw set unnaturally.

"You tell me this tremendously personal thing as though I were nobody, a mere functionary."

It was true. Meg did not deny it to herself. She had this thought: Matter spins into a particular combination on a particular day—champagne grapes on a china plate, a fire made from compressed wood, a gingham-covered basket—and their convergence unleashes Meg's cruelty.

When Charlotte's salad arrived, Meg cut into her lamb but found she could not easily swallow. Her throat was constricted.

She dared to look at Charlotte, to see if she observed the difficulty, then regretted it when her eyes quickly welled up. She looked down again.

"Do you think I'm a monster? Do you think I'll say one word against this adoption, now that I see what it means to you?"

"It's fine about the money. We can certainly get by without it."

"You are so matter-of-fact. You couldn't possibly feel so cold about this. Where is Kimble now? Who is taking care of her?"

"She's at a foster home. Under Social Services. They have people who take kids on an emergency basis. She's fine. I spoke with her."

"A foster home! How did she end up in a foster home? Terrible things can happen in those homes. You see the news, Meg."

"What was I supposed to do, kidnap her? I had to go through channels. Nothing terrible will happen. I spoke with her. She was at the Central Park Zoo."

Charlotte was silent while she finished her salad. Then she said, "This is a great concern."

"No, it's not," said Meg firmly. Because Kimble was suddenly in Charlotte's life, her welfare was now an urgent priority. Pure acquisitiveness. One thing, one person grows precious as countless others rot.

"Then why are we discussing it?" Charlotte started on her tuna. "You probably think I care about where Kimble came from, but I don't."

"I know you don't," lied Meg. "Remember, she has a grandmother. Her mother's mother lives in Queens. It is important that I preserve that relationship."

"Yes, I think it's very important." Charlotte cut into the grilled tuna.

"I guess you'll be a grandmother of sorts too."

Charlotte rearranged some baby lima beans on her plate. She did not smile, but her face softened. "I suppose in this new world of ours, you could say that I will be."

"Do you think the new world is unworthy of the old one?"

"I didn't say that. Years ago Daddy said you would make a good prosecutor. I thought, No, you were too timid. Now I see what he meant."

"Do you know that I have been deliberating and deliberating about whether I should adopt Kimble, and one of the things that gave me pause was what you would tell your friends?"

"That's your problem," snapped Charlotte with such alacrity the popover girl looked up from the other side of the fireplace.

Silence. Meg looked at her plate, but only the parsley remained there. "I'm sorry. But you haven't exactly surrounded me with support and enlightenment. You never ask me a thing about my life."

Libby leaped to mind unbidden. "Prospecting for things of no value again," she had said. "Things you don't even want. You *want* her to ask about your life? What do you want to tell her?"

"Meg," Charlotte asked now, "are you really such a hothouse orchid? Can you really not survive outside of a completely hospitable environment?"

"Don't lecture me about adversity. Please. And by the way, when are you going to Estoril? Or Majorca?"

Charlotte continued eating slowly. "All my friends have had trouble of one kind or another with their children," she confided. "None of them have had unruffled relationships, I assure you. But I don't believe one has a son or daughter, certainly not one of your age, who resents them for having provided a high standard of living. I see what is happening to our economy, Meg. I see where we're headed. What would you like me to do, divest myself completely and take a cup down to the Bowery? What good would that do?"

"Please stop talking to me as though I were 15," said Meg.

"I will say this," Charlotte added. "One thing my friends and I have all observed. The people of your generation have not grown into adults. Not like the people of ours. I don't know why this is."

Meg was oddly comforted by Charlotte's words. She was afraid her mother took the position that Meg had not grown up because she was gay. If she had not matured to her mother's standards, at least she was merely part of an evolutionary phenomenon.

"It depends on your definition of 'adult,'" began Meg.

"Adults in my day drew clear lines between their private and public selves," said Charlotte. "I know you pooh-pooh this whole notion. The fact remains, Meg: There were lines then, and everyone respected them. My friends and I did not peel back each other's layers. There was a regard for privacy that gave us some mystery, some remote dignity. You find this wanting; I find it desirable. Society is interested in our capable performance, not our underwear. Would you like some dessert?"

"No, thanks." Now Meg tinkered with the tiny silver tongs set in the sugar bowl. She thought about Charlotte's capable performance in the world. She and her friends had always been in motion around their children, directing their development with a ferocity that was never spent, a razor-sharp focus they encouraged in each other. They pooled the resource of their time to surround their children with their set, and sometimes overwrought, expressions; they were in the audience of recitals, in the bleachers lining gymnastic performances, behind the scenes at school and community board meetings. When their children were grown these women smoothly shifted courses to aid a thousand social and cultural causes, but never, Meg had observed, political ones. Meg wondered if some recent idle moments had disclosed a few revelations among the members of her mother's circle: the mistress flown down to St. Croix, the wife begging for a household allowance. What remained hidden? For the sake of maintaining some mystery, some remote dignity, what further injuries would never seek comfort?

"We're veering off the point," continued Charlotte. "The point is you are adopting a child, and you're trying to decide if I will play a role. I can understand that. This is, as you say, not a usual situation."

As Charlotte spoke, the young businessmen at the next table grew increasingly voluble. Meg could no longer hear her mother. Charlotte cast them a cold glance, which did not have the slightest effect.

"Shall we?" asked Charlotte, and raised her hand to get the waiter's attention. Meg disliked this gesture—yet often used it herself.

Outside, the snow had stopped falling. Whatever traces had been on the ground had disappeared under people's footsteps. Without agreeing on a plan, Meg and Charlotte began to walk west, then turned south on Fifth Avenue. As they walked, Charlotte commented on the new coats of passersby, women who could be her neighbors. Then she asked Meg if she had any pots in her current inventory, perhaps one or two with an unnoticeable chip, that might be good for Juliet Tree. She said she would be happy to purchase one. She said that, actually, now that she thought about it, there was an account left from Steven's estate: a plain, nothing savings account from a bank in Illinois that she had never turned into an investment. She could draw on money from this account to buy a pot for Juliet in an amount that one might pay for a small pot by, say, Noguchi. That way, Charlotte said, Meg could keep the money and have her time alone with Kimble and feel a little like Noguchi in the bargain.

"Take it!" Meg could hear Libby cheering. "Take it and run; she'll never offer it again."

"How about this?" asked Meg. "How about I throw a custom pot for Juliet, even though I can't stand the woman, and you pay me what you would pay for a Noguchi, but I'll pay you back at 9 percent interest by next summer?"

"I will pay you what I would pay for a Noguchi, and you'll repay me whenever you can at no interest," concluded Charlotte. "At least you'll manage not to insult me while you're asserting your pride."

They had come upon B. Altman's—closed, dark, its windows bleakly reflecting the colorless winter avenue. It struck Meg that the closing of B. Altman's was truly a loss to the city, to some pulsing sense of good cheer on mid Fifth Avenue. One less place, Meg reflected, for her mother to seek refuge, one less bazaar of color and fragrance, of rich material and ornate design to ease Charlotte's nerves when the idle moments mounted—threatening, perhaps, to overturn the mystery she had crafted, the dignity she would not be ashamed to hear described as "remote."

A wind howled up the avenue. Meg hunched her shoulders inside her new bomber jacket. She watched as Charlotte peered in the darkened windows. "It really *is* a shame," she shouted above the wind. She put her arm around her mother's shoulder. Leather dropped into deep-brown mink. "A real loss to the city."

"Oh, it was an anachronism," dismissed Charlotte. "All the department stores are now. I'm not sorry to see them go. Now, if you'll excuse me, I'm going to hail this cab and go home and sink into a nice hot tub. I've been around the world, but my considered opinion is, there's no place like a nice hot tub."

15

Back from the Snowy Egret, Meg reinforced a fallen strip of insulation around her risers, opened some mail, turned on the phone machine, and heard, "Yes, hello. This is Libby Zindel's daughter calling. Please call me back when you can at her apartment. Thank you."

Even as Meg instantly realized Libby was dead, she had this disorienting and quivering thought: The voice on the machine could not be Libby's daughter, because *she* was Libby's daughter. She promptly recovered herself and called the apartment. "I'm Meg Krantz," she said, her tone almost a dare. She waited to hear the words, then heard them. She did not ask the real daughter's name but thanked her for calling during what must be a terrible, chaotic time. She wrote down "Ethical Culture Society, 10 A.M., Tuesday," repeated her thank-you, and hung up.

Meg busied herself about the loft, first setting the Kimble pot on the floor where the dresser would go, then taping the seams between the drywall panels of the new closet. That done, she tacked several paint swatches to the plaster board. For many minutes Meg advanced and retreated on these swatches, trying to discern the difference between apricot blush and apricot blush tint. The difference was too negligible for her eye. This was a defeat, for she was suddenly desperate to visualize the large expanse from the tiny specimen. The color she would paint the closet tomorrow had to come out as precisely as she anticipated it today.

Meg went to bed before the moon came up. She saw only Libby when she closed her eyes, a woman Meg was not permitted—for all of Libby's unorthodoxy—to really know, a woman she *paid* not to know. Beyond the great shame, the great mendacity of this, was the dread that she might not know herself with Libby gone. She stayed awake all night. At first she lay in bed. Then, in the deepest part of night, she got up and wandered about her loft, finally stopping at one of the huge north windows. Through the glass and unbroken lace of chicken wire, she watched a raging homeless man pace back and forth at the entrance to Duane Street, the headlights of Hudson Street traffic illuminating and then eclipsing him until he was himself transformed into a light that flashed steadily off and on.

∞   ∞   ∞

Tuesday, 9:45 A.M. Two days before, Meg had painted Kimble's closet apricot blush tint, an oil-based paint that she had bought in error but had been too tired to return. As Meg entered the Ethical Culture Society on 64th Street, stroking her chin as she stopped to check the building, the smell of the mineral spirits she had scrubbed with that morning overpowered the Chanel No. 19 on her wrists.

People were gathered in the lobby. Meg did not know if they were there for Libby or for something else. There were

morning lectures, Meg had heard, on humanist themes. There
were support groups. Meg stood for a moment by a potted ficus
tree next to the door. She heard organ music; it swelled, then
stopped suddenly. This lobby was long and narrow, an anteroom
to something vast beyond, but a room on its own account, with
leaded sconces and polished floors. The people who milled
about were dressed as Upper West Siders on any other day—
casual, hip, jewelry suggestive of Guatemala and of Nigeria.
Some people wore gray; no one wore black. Today was warmer
than Saturday, when Meg had met Charlotte. Beneath her
leather jacket she wore a new rayon tunic, in a color called cas-
sis, and her Sanskrit scarf. Meg was readjusting this scarf when
a woman not five feet in front of her let out a loud sob, then
flinched as if she might be struck, and clapped her hand over
her mouth. Meg recognized the woman. She had emerged from
Libby's apartment the first time Meg had gone there. She was
a former customer, now like Meg herself. A young man with red
hair and rosy fingertips began to embrace her, then thought better of it and placed his hand stiffly on her shoulder. The outside
door opened, and these two were joined immediately by two
women. One was heavy and wore a crushed-velvet cape; the
other was thin with wild, coarse hair and a dissipated look, as if
she had just managed her way from an after-hours club or a
stranger's bed. The four of them greeted each other by grasping
hands, nodding, staring at one another. Meg realized they were
members of Libby's group, a group that had disbanded seven or
eight months before Meg had begun to see Libby, a group Libby
had shamelessly called her "brood." Several times she had told
Meg it was a pity her brood had graduated to, as she put it,
"unbolstered reality," for Meg would have made a fine contri-
bution. This had always surprised Meg, who had no appreciation of herself as someone who could enlighten others, who in

fact thought her small facility of expression flowered only in one-on-one encounters: in someone's bed, in booths at Greek coffee shops, across from Libby Zindel.

A man of about 40 entered through the main door now and identified the group. Even before he reached them he said, "This is one little reunion we could have done without."

"Obviously, Harold," said the woman who had sobbed.

A muscle twitched in the face of the man with rosy finger-tips. "How are you, Harold?"

"Fine, considering. How are you all?"

"We all suck," answered the dissipated one. "What do you think? I knew she was sick, but I didn't know how sick. Did you, Gina?" she asked, turning to the one in the crushed-velvet cape.

"I didn't know anything till the daughter called me," said Gina. "Imagine being her daughter. I mean, her *real* daughter. Who in New York City is qualified to exorcise you if you're *Libby's* daughter?"

"Don't you think the essence of Libby is that if you're her daughter you don't have to be exorcised?" asked the red-haired man.

"No!" declared two women at the same time. One of them turned away and looked at Meg, who had been staring. Caught off-guard, she smiled compatibly.

The more this group brought Libby into a recognizable light, the more Meg wanted to withdraw, to disassociate her-self from their words. Sometimes it was only through the act of withdrawing that Meg could perceive her own experience as precious, as singular. This morning, surrounded by versions of a self she had never cultivated, a self that sought comfort by speaking every word aloud, she wanted only to recede. She removed her jacket and started to walk to the inside doors someone had opened. (As she passed the group, she wondered if now, with Libby gone, the legacy of Charlotte's temperament might catch up with her. Would she begin to eschew intimate exchanges and adopt a pose of remote dignity?) She heard the sobbing one whisper, "Is that the daughter? Did I fuck up again?"

The huge room inside, Meg thought, was something between a sanctuary and an auditorium. It was paneled in dark wood, walnut or mahogany, and the carpet was a deep red. Carved into the wood around the stage were the words THE PLACE WHERE PEOPLE MEET TO SEEK THE HIGHEST GROUND. Meg studied these words. Libby had no romance about the highest ground. Libby boasted of spending gray weekday afternoons in bed with a pint of Häagen-Dazs and the talk shows. The highest ground, Meg decided, was the daughter's province. Meg wondered if the wood above the stage had always held those words, or if they had replaced THE PLACE WHERE MEN MEET TO SEEK THE HIGHEST GROUND after some commotion had been made.

Organ music, noticeably tentative, continued to play. Some people were seated; others stood in a cluster near the first row of seats. At the front of the room, below the speaking platform, were two enormous sprays of mixed flowers, their colors too hastily considered, a discordant blend whose proclamation was neither stately nor renascent. Between these flowers stood a woman about Meg's age who was undoubtedly the daughter. She accepted people's condolences with a strained expression, as Meg imagined she herself would, struggling to maintain the requisite tiny smile, the smile that gave people permission to say their piece, the smile that recorded her as just barely, just sufficiently, within the room of her mother's memorial. She wore a Christian Dior scarf, one Meg recognized from Charlotte's wardrobe. She resembled Libby, yet her presentation was more studied. Her makeup was applied more emphatically, and there was about her, particularly about her high brow and her arched back and taut shoulders, a certain toughness—a decidedly feminine toughness, the admirable fortitude of a '40s businesswoman.

Beside this woman who had identified herself only as "Libby Zindel's daughter" was the granddaughter whose Girl Scout cookies Libby had hawked last spring. It was not easy to associate this girl with the stiff, reproachless uniform and ugly merit badges of an American Girl Scout. With some effort, Meg could imagine the granddaughter's younger self as a Brownie, her beanie set defiantly askew, but a Girl Scout was out of the question. She stood there in her shiny leggings, the sleeves of her sweater dangling beyond the tips of her fingers, staring at people and periodically snapping back her head, chasing her long bangs to the side. Her costume, next to that of her mother, was a testament only to their struggles for dominance, and if this girl had remained a Girl Scout despite her appearance here this morning, in these clothes, it spoke volumes about Libby's daughter. Meg wondered what the preceding few days had been like for the granddaughter, for she imagined that she had adopted her phlegmatic manner unthinkingly, a handy and reliable defense.

Meg found herself an aisle seat, laid down her jacket, and began her way to the daughter. As Libby would have instructed in her uncompromising way, "Be an adult! It's a charade, but it'll make you feel better. Take my word for it."

Meg took small steps behind the people in front of her, a man and woman about Libby's age who looked exhausted, truly afflicted. Meg walked as softly as she could. When she finally reached the daughter, she said, "I'm Meg Krantz. Thank you for calling me."

"Oh, yes, of course," said the daughter, who clearly had no idea who Meg was. "Yes, I'm Susan. Your presence is very much appreciated. This is my daughter, Diane."

"Hello, Diane," said Meg. (Susan? Diane? These were not names for Libby's daughter and granddaughter.) "I'm so sorry for you. You know, your grandmother loved helping you sell your cookies."

To her embarrassment, Meg felt her eyes sting with tears, a response to her own sentimental and irrelevant remark. Diane just glared at her. Finally she said, "I guess."

Neither Susan nor Diane asked Meg how she had known Libby; it was taken for granted.

Susan had already turned to receive the next person in line when Meg touched her sleeve. In response, Susan turned back, her eyes wide open in expectation of vital news, a look that caused Meg to lower her voice. "Is there somewhere in particular to send donations?"

"Yes. We've set up a memorial fund here at the Society. Thank you for asking."

Meg nodded and found herself faced again with Diane, her hand now on her hip, the heel of one shoe pressed against the instep of the other, an effete pose she took for sophistication.

"Take care of yourself," advised Meg.

As she passed Diane again, she was alarmed at how completely she felt herself transformed into a child—not a woman younger than Susan but a child younger than Diane, her own body suddenly awkward, her own clothes now ill-fitting, the space around her grown close, a challenge to negotiate. Making her way back to her seat, Meg longed only to describe this feeling to Libby. Libby would nod as only she could: little bows that gained force and momentum like applause, a rocking motion that contained the solemnity of worship. Meg would not hold back, even though it had been Libby's family who had so reduced her. She who had sat in Libby's blue recliner, sometimes hugging a bright, crocheted afghan, pointing out the patchiness of her own character—whole areas never filled in, recognizably fallow and neglected areas that caused her shame year after year. She would complain that the composure of Libby's own daughter had unnerved her, had rendered her grief ungainly.

Back at her seat, Meg prepared to listen to whatever would be said. Again she looked around. She looked at the wooden figures carved into the walls (philosophers, Meg supposed, surely not apostles), at the huge brass ring suspended from the ceiling, a light fixture set again with leading and with milky glass, at the ruby-red of the stained glass at the rear of the room. Maybe Libby had belonged here after all, for wasn't it incumbent upon humanists to tolerate the irreverent in their midst?

A man in a dark-gray suit stepped up to a podium, drank from a glass of water tucked out of sight, gazed out at the audience and said, "It is ourselves or nothing in this world. Libby Zindel knew this, *lived* this."

Meg craned forward to listen, but something resolute within her, a mighty devotion to her Libby, a Libby who had nothing to do with this room or anyone in it, shielded her from his words, cast his words into a drone. Where was Libby now, was all Meg could wonder. She would be cremated. Meg knew this because Libby had told her months earlier, before there was any question of illness. "Nobody's getting my organs either!" she had snapped. "How do I know my pancreas won't end up inside the body of some mealy-mouthed, bigoted little dick? They fly those organs all over the country, you know. I think it's a sideline of Sky Chef. *My* pancreas, who shares my politics and everything else—who knows where it could end up! I may not be in control of diddly-shit in this world, but I can at least control the fate of my body parts."

"We determine how we live and how we live influences others. Libby Zindel knew this above all else," continued the speaker.

Meg focused her thoughts only on Libby's ashes. She had never seen crematory ashes. Her father had been buried in a plot in Westchester, not far from their country club. Were the ashes black and curled, like cinders from a bonfire, or small and densely packed, like cigarette ashes? Did they contain bone chips tiny as granules, or were they light as flour dust? How could Libby—whom Meg had believed would soon call to announce she was taking customers again—how could she possibly be ashes in an urn, awaiting delivery or disposal? How was it possible that Libby—who had repeatedly inched up to the edge of her seat to attend to Meg's every word, to dispense crucial advice, to insist that there were decisions in life that redeemed people—how was it possible that this Libby was now a drift of ashes in an urn?

Minutes later—exiting onto 64th Street, her body tingling from the effort to keep herself in check, her steps hesitant—Meg clung behind the group, the brood. She inhaled the charged air of their bond. She wanted to know them. She wanted to go where they went. When Harold boomed "I can't believe the daughter looks like a goddamned Republican," Meg answered, "a goddamned Junior *League* Republican."

16

The Greek goddess Hera was the fiery, jealous protectress of women and was the goddess who presided over marriage and childbirth. In Meg's view, Hera was the right goddess for Juliet Tree. Hera gave life to Ares and his twin sister Eris when she touched a flower, and to Hebe when she touched a lettuce leaf. Children by parthenogenesis. Meg admired Hera's independence from the unfaithful Zeus. And she preferred to think of Juliet Tree touching a flower or a head of lettuce, rather than the prick of the canny lawyer who had robbed her of her White Plains house.

Back from the funeral, Meg changed out of her new tunic blouse and sat down at her studio table, a Formica-covered door affixed to sawhorses. Although she had been quick to correct Charlotte that she threw rather than sculpted her pots, this one she planned to hand-build. She removed from her boom box a tape by the children's songwriter Raffi, replaced it with Glenn Gould's *Goldberg Variations*, and began to sandwich-slice a large block of clay. She scattered dampened filler between the slices and quickly—with a muscular exertion that felt good, that even after years of repetition made her feel vigorous and capable—began to knead and wedge the clay. For this activity she wore a Brooks Brothers shirt she had recently salvaged from her father's closet, a closet full of shirts and suits that Charlotte had never sorted through, an entire wardrobe that had acquired the soft brittleness of clothes in disuse.

First, Meg made the pot's base—a disc of clay, which she flattened from a ball with her palm. She cut it around a template and then checked carefully for evenness. She set the perfect base on a round cutting board.

Meg had a favorite method for throwing and another for coiling, but she had relied upon both for so many years that she could no longer discern the refinement of feeling that made each pot unique. Her work was valued for the involvement of her hand, yet Meg had come to think of her hand as a tool of mass production.

She paused for a moment to listen to the Gould tape, an old favorite of Sarina's. Amazing that after all the time that had passed since their first months together, after all the evidence she had collected that Sarina's character was slight, undeserving of her serious attention, Meg still clung to that first, elevated vision of her. Funny, thought Meg, kneading more gently now, how people are driven to deify unworthy heroes. When they see their earthly failings (Hera was a tormentor, Sarina a liar), they banish them to unseen distances from where they can idealize them all the more.

Turning up the volume of the tape player, Meg moved to sit on the concrete floor and begin shaping her first coil. First, she slapped down some clay and squeezed out a rough sausage shape, then she rolled it along a smooth board—at first gently, next with more pressure to elongate it. She stopped to check for a uniform diameter along the coil's length—these days a near certain achievement. There she sat with her legs outspread, rolling and squeezing in the air or along the board in the way of the native New Guinea potters. But this posture shortly gave her back pains and hampered her control, so she conceded to standing at her table. Her coils were not as long as those of the famous New Guinea potters, but they were utterly precise. She rolled and listened to the music and thought, as she had many times before, how easy it was to bring goddesses into the lives of women who yearned for them, women who managed mutual funds by day and descended upon magical thoughts at night.

Soon it was time to build over the prepared base. Meg placed a coil on its rim with one hand and guided it with the other. Her fingers kept working along the rim, squeezing and binding. When the ring was complete she broke off the coil and began again. Repeatedly she wrapped the coils and pinched off their ends until the pot had achieved some height, some fullness. The repetition, when it worked, became a process of enchantment. Only this enchanted repetition could make the pot something more than a pot. Yet this afternoon, rolling and wrapping the coils, Meg felt nothing. She merely executed a performance. She thought about the White Plains house filled with abominable plastic toys and the voice of Juliet Tree herself, a voice in constant complaint, a voice buoyed on an undertone of effrontery. This pot, she knew, would be placed on a chrome-and-glass table next to the latest Danielle Steel. It would be filled with miniature Tootsie Rolls for the children. They would be told to reach in carefully because the pot, no matter what they all might think of it, had brought them the new baby.

Meg wanted to borrow something from the piano music filling her loft but found nothing in it for this moment. Then, as she bonded the coils by dragging her thumb from top to bottom, inside and out, her thumb an instrument of unvarying pressure, it came to her. This pot would not be for Juliet Tree: It would be for Libby Zindel, an urn for the ashes Meg would never see—it would become, in the most palpable sense, Meg holding Libby. Defined entirely by its high purpose, this pot would be exquisite, and when Meg presented it to Charlotte in fulfillment of their arrangement, Libby would be inside, congratulating Meg on the elegance, the pure adultness, of her deception.

Now Meg became a conjurer, her thumb a divining rod. Each new coil she would pull down to the partly formed pot by rotating the cutting board on which it was mounted, a circle that she insisted be musical. When the pot achieved its basic shape, a pleasing bulge that curved up to a sturdy neck, Meg stopped, replaced the Glenn Gould tape with an old Philip Glass composition, *Glassworks,* and began to coil again—this time unconcerned with precision, forcing a shape narrower but taller than the base, a shape that angled back to balance daringly off the neck.

For the first time in years, Meg worked deep into the morning hours. The shape she had fit to the pot's neck and tilted toward the sky became Hera's head. By adding pellets and small slabs of clay, Meg molded the features that suggested both Hera's maternity and her assured sense of command. Assuming her role in the culture, Meg's Hera was comely, yet there was a restlessness about her, as if she might buck a restraint and then become wild.

Carefully, Meg scraped away the thumb marks on Hera's body and head, around and over her features, both inside and out, giving her an entirely smooth surface. Then she coiled again, this time wrapping the shapes carelessly and binding with a heavy, deliberate touch. This was Hera's untended hair. Meg left the coils uneven but erased their texture with a metal scraper. Mounted around Hera's head, this hair was the pot's wide rim.

Finally, using slender pellets and incisions like the Ibibio potters of Nigeria, Meg decorated the widest part of the pot with a motif—a flower yielding a tiny human figure, an unabashedly sentimental image that Meg knew Libby would love for its kitschiness.

Later Meg would highlight the texture of this motif by brushing it over with a diluted glaze. The inside she would fully glaze, and then she would fire the pot to a stoneware temperature. For now, though, the loft fully bright with morning, Meg walked off to her bed, drew the covers over her head, and cried for Libby. Of course Libby's ashes would never lie inside the new pot. Meg knew, in fact, that there would be no ashes: Her daughter Susan would leave instructions for their disposal. She would suffer for years for having done so, but in the required moment, Meg imagined Susan would simply tell the undertaker to follow whatever procedure was necessary; she was not the morbid type who saved ashes.

∞   ∞   ∞

The following day there was a birthday party for Ray in the REACH playroom. Another pediatric volunteer had called Meg an hour before the party was to begin, told her it had been thrown together spontaneously. Meg was certain this was not true. The entire agency had worried that this would be Ray's last birthday; the party had been scrupulously planned. Her inclusion was another matter. Meg guessed that Tina was against her attending. There was no way Meg would miss this party. The volunteer had told her it would be held in a playroom vacated of children, the ultimate present to Ray. Meg had hastily wrapped up two ceramic mugs. She had run down to the corner flower shop for a dozen roses. Her presents, she knew, would be the least considered, the least personal. There would be staff members who either knew the tiniest details about Ray or who were talented gift givers, the kind who could reflect back to complete strangers their most unique qualities.

When Meg entered the playroom, she almost turned out again. All the toys and books, the air mattresses, and the colorful rubber matting had been removed. So had been the posters from the Children's Book Council. In their place were REACH's most graphic safer-sex posters, recouped from the days when there were no heterosexual donors of significance. Some of the posters must have been retrieved from the archives. Viewed together in one room, they created a chorus of defiance: *With this sheath of rubber I shall do everything you always despised me for*. On the table, Fiestaware was stacked between fans of linen napkins. Within the curve of each fan was an expensive cake, small but high and dense: chocolate mousse with apricot filling, carrot with vanilla icing. There were orchids in crystal vases. The presents stacked on either side of the table were wrapped in thin rice paper, glitter paper, or hand-stenciled crepe. They were tied with supple strips of bark or multicolored ribbons shedding curly tendrils. Meg was loathe to put down her quickly wrapped mugs beside the other presents. She wished she had picked up one of those glossy gift bags with an Impressionist painting reproduced along its four sides. She stood with her wrists crossed behind her back, the wrapped cups awkwardly nestled in her grip, her fingers aching from the strain.

Barely after Meg's arrival, Ray walked into the room. He had been on an early lunch break, though it was clear he had spent it doing battle—doubtlessly the sort that was routine for

REACH staffers: maybe trying to reason with a line worker
from the Division of AIDS Services or from Disability, someone
trying to block one of his client's services. As he entered the
room, he was cursing. Meg reared back slightly when she saw
his face. It had taken on a faint purplish hue that could have
been part temper and part the pentamidine that he took every
week to prevent PCP. His color made his anger all the more for-
midable, and yet oddly visible right beneath was the pallor that
accompanied a new gauntness. Meg was startled that Ray's eyes
since she had last seen him had taken on a ghostly stare. A
damp cloudiness seemed to spill beyond the perimeters of his
actual eyes. Now it seemed clear as Ray pushed himself from
the corridor into the playroom that he was cursing his own pain.
It was a moment of total release, a luxury he allowed himself in
an unwatched moment. Yet as he entered the playroom 40 people, noisemakers in hand, had their heads turned in his direction. There was no recourse for the party givers but to put the
plastic mouthpieces to their lips as quickly as possible, to blow
as hard as they could, sending waxy paper furls flying out erect,
their screeches like a keening.

When people put aside their noisemakers and began, hesi-
tantly, to clap, Meg watched Ray marshal his forces. This was
an entirely manifest process. His head and shoulders trembled,
the effect of the surprise on his weak body. His rhinestone earring shook and glittered beside his gray cheek. As he tried to
smile his dry lips stretched taut. There was a tiny fleck of spit-
tle at the corner of his mouth, a bit of the wake of some med-
ication. "You guys," he said. "And women," he added, looking at
Meg and, on the other side, at Tina and several others. "That's
W-O-M-Y-N, for those who would prefer it."

Everyone laughed inordinately. Bill from the recreation department emerged from the crowd to kiss Ray. It was immediately clear

that this was a mistake. Ray had to brace himself for the abrupt-
ness of the unplanned contact, a kiss as a blow, its warmth sub-
verted by its considerable force. Bill smiled wanly. No one else
approached Ray. Several people blew again on their noisemakers.
Plastic bottles of flavored seltzer were opened. Tina began to cut
the mousse cake, all the while talking about how the only way to
manage a career at REACH was to charge as many fucking
gourmet cakes to petty cash as possible.

Ray began to relax. An observer might have attributed his
vague and misty eyes to sentimentality rather than his inability
to focus on the solid objects before him. After Ray had trouble
opening his first present, everyone in the room took up his or
her own present and opened it for him. There were CDs by
Italian divas, Broadway tickets, a Raku pot, a key chain from
Tiffany's. People in the financial department had chipped in to
give Ray and his lover a midnight supper cruise around
Manhattan. There were none of the usual gifts of silk jockeys
and passes for exclusive after-hours clubs. The posters around
the room might have been out of place, but Meg was happy to
catch Ray smiling at one of a black man with oiled muscles
rolling back a condom. She was relieved, too, that she got to
unwrap her mugs unceremoniously, to approach Ray quietly.
"These are humble," she said, "but they are truly from the
hearth. One for you and one for your lover."

Ray took up one of the mugs and turned it around. He lifted it and smiled at Meg's initials scrawled with brown glaze into
the bottom of the mug. "I'd hate to read your chart notes," he
said.

"Don't worry, no one will ever have to again."

"I wouldn't be so sure," said Ray. "History makes circles
around here faster than it does in most places."

Meg laughed. "I probably won't have time to volunteer," she

said. "Keeping up my business and taking care of Kimble...I can't imagine a free moment."

Ray only nodded. He looked exhausted. It had been a long time, years really, since Meg had taken up the point of view that she should censor herself in the presence of someone dying. Her experience with one client after another had proved that the more she restrained herself out of a sense of propriety, the more undeliverable was her true service: the evidence she could provide that life proceeded unaltered, full of the trivia that subdued the dying person's terrors, full even of hasty, tactless allusions to the future and to activities that depended on robust health. Yet now she cursed herself for not showing more restraint. She had as much as told Ray that her volunteering, that people's dying, was her hobby. "Maybe when Kimble's in kindergarten or first grade," she added, "I can go back." And for this she blushed deeply, for this was worse. Ray would not be here when Kimble was in kindergarten. What did he care what she did in two, two-and-a-half years?

Ray kept looking at the mug. "Thank you for these. I'm sure Doug and I will enjoy them. I'll drink my vile brews, and he'll sit across from me with his freshly ground hazelnut coffee. Just cause for murder, don't you think?"

Meg wanted so much to kiss Ray, to hold him. Rather, she laid a hand on his shoulder. She withheld the natural firmness of her grip, created the touch of a different, less resolute person than herself. He brushed this hand with his cheek. "There are so many just causes for murder," she said. "It's for good reason I don't arm myself."

17

An hour after the party for Ray, as Meg was bundling the finished, glazed Hera in bubble wrap, preparing to deliver her to Charlotte uptown, Consuela Soto called. Meg found herself in a terror of anticipation. By immediate impulse she began to speak fast, her words falling and building upon one another, a wall against the coming message. "Have you seen Ray lately? The playroom director at REACH? I just came from his birthday party. They threw him this great party...." Meg wanted to tell Consuela everything but stopped herself. What made her think Consuela knew about Ray? And now, surely Consuela made note of Meg's lack of focus, of her silly patter at a crucial time.

"Ray's a sweetie, isn't he?" Consuela said. "We've never met face-to-face. One of those warm and cozy phone relationships. Better than the in-the-flesh kind sometimes."

Oh, thought Meg, *she understands. People have swerved away like this before.* She waited.

"I was in family court yesterday afternoon," said Consuela. "We have arranged to put Kimble Toffler in your custodial care with a temporary license. As we talked about, you'll get a Title 19 card for her medical care. If you're interested in adopting, I suggest you get the wheels rolling right away. We are obligated to list her as free for adoption even though she is in your care. Now, remember, the state child welfare system is run also by counties. Our county is so high-volume we have to contract out all our adoptions. We work with several agencies. Jewish Board is a big one. We would probably direct them to effect the adoption."

All of this was delivered in such a businesslike tone that Meg was afraid any contrasting tone of hers would put a burden on the moment. "So you think I should contact them?" she asked, having barely heard Consuela's last words. She hoped she was making a reasonable connection.

"Yes, or one of the other agencies. Mrs. Cheney can tell you the others. Now, of course we know about Kimble's grandmother. You should know that we couldn't find her in our system, but she did call to recommend you as the guardian. Are there any other relatives?"

"Not to my knowledge."

"Good, because it doesn't matter how distant a relative is. If they're blood, they have power. And before a final adoption takes place we have to send them certified letters, and we also run an ad in the paper warning any relatives that an adoption is in the works. I just think you should know this, because there's a legal risk as long as relatives are around."

This was harsh news, particularly because Meg had avoided thinking about it herself. Over the past months she had been so busy dealing with the obstacles within her reach she had not considered the ones beyond it. Kimble might have blood relatives on Barry's side. What assurance did Meg have that they would not come forward, maybe in frightening numbers, once Kimble's imminent adoption was made public? Well, thought Meg in a rushed-up moment she could not control, they're probably all crack heads and prostitutes; they probably all have records.

"Shirley Marzola tells me that Kimble doesn't have any other relatives," Meg said. "I think there's only a great-aunt in a nursing home in the Bronx. But thank you for explaining the procedure to me. How soon before I can get Kimble?"

"I just need to let you know, Ms. Krantz, for the record, that any complaint of neglect that comes into the field office results in the child being removed from the home. That said, on to the part you want to hear. Mrs. Cheney can bring her over in the next few hours."

It had been more than a week since Meg had seen Mrs. Cheney. The report of the home study was supposed to be completed within 24 hours; the family court date was scheduled the next day. Meg knew how procedures at REACH stretched out beyond their projected deadlines; she had assumed the city to be even less attentive to schedules. She had called Consuela's office once and was told by a clerk that the court docket was spilling over these days, there was nothing to be done about it. Maybe it was a good thing that so much had happened in the week since Mrs. Cheney's visit, otherwise Meg would surely have made a nuisance of herself, calling every second day. This week, though, had been one of those times when the pace of events outstripped Meg's ability to consider them. It occurred to Meg, not for the first time, that by adopting Kimble she was choosing event over reflection. In the years ahead, events would collide into one another. She would reflect upon them when she was old.

"Oh, please! By all means, ask Mrs. Cheney to bring her over as soon as she can!" Meg did not try to control her voice. Her tone was brimming.

"She's still way up in the Bronx, so it'll take a bit. I do wish you fine luck, Ms. Krantz. In the best of all worlds, this will be an opportunity for the child and for you."

"You and Ray have both been wonderful," said Meg. "You may have never met, but you make a great team." Meg said this, and then she stayed on the line, waiting for no reason. She pictured Consuela Soto just as she had seen her, the lustrous gold threads of her shawl wheeling through that drab waiting room with its broken fiberglass chairs and its positively dead plant wrapped in a bow.

As soon as Meg was off the phone, a storm of energy overcame her, its ascent so sudden she felt herself balanced precariously on top. Energy meant to be contained within her had escaped; she was an afterthought bobbing along its surface, dispensable to a general tide of forward movement. She looked about the loft. It took her an eternity to recall that she had been in the middle of wrapping Hera, the finished Hera, whose swollen belly was decorated with its parade of flowers yielding tiny figures. It would be impossible to return to Hera. Should she call someone: Charlotte, Ray, even Sarina? She could call two or three of her fellow REACH volunteers, or Chris downstairs. She could even call Cami. No. All would congratulate her in a cordial tone that would leave her disgruntled.

Meg rushed to the window. The sky was gray. Snow flurries fell slowly, then were driven to a slant by a gust of wind. Meg knew she should busy herself preparing for Kimble's arrival, but she could not imagine any act of preparation that would absorb this sudden, unruly vigor. As quickly as she could, she changed to her winter running clothes: thermal leggings, silk underwear, T-shirt, sweatshirt, ski band. With nothing but her keys in her hand, she ran out the door to the elevator, now covered top-to-bottom with somber religious paintings. Once on West Street,

Meg started running uptown. It was a weekday, and few people were around. Those she saw might have been local merchants on lunch break, artists on errands, men trying their luck off hours at the piers. No one got in her way; Meg's new energy vanquished everyone from her orbit. It was a graced run. During this run she had no body, no heaviness to remind her she was corporeal. The run was fueled by victory and, she knew, melodrama, for she indulged herself in the thought that this would be her last run. As she flew into the West Village past Bank and Jane streets, past restaurants that would not open before dinner and stores with funny, improbable themes, she saw before her a clear and wonderful opportunity for change. All the way up to 14th Street she saw how easily she might assume her new responsibilities, how she might at last and unhesitatingly seek what she had for years avoided. Why couldn't she open a retail store along these very streets? Not only would she keep her long-standing accounts and her mail-order business, but she would have off-the-street trade as well. She would hire a part-time assistant from 3 to 8, someone to make money for her while she tended Kimble after school. She and an assistant (eventually, maybe, a partner) would alternate doing trade shows. When Meg exhibited, Kimble would accompany her, would grow up at ease with the public and with meeting new children in new places. In two or three years there might easily be another store. She would exhibit and sell the work of other potters, fly with Kimble to Japan to take workshops from master potters, teach in a well-equipped studio in the back of one of her stores. As Meg circled 14th Street and began to head downtown, this plan was clear and shapely, a perfect form secured by its timely conception.

Headed toward home, the burdens of her body returned. The steady flurries had accumulated at the collar of her sweatshirt, creating a freezing band around her neck. She had not done warm-up stretches, and as her feet pounded the pavement she felt a stiffness in her calves. The tops of her thighs began to ache. The contours of her plan began to lose their crisp edges. Kimble would be with her in a few short hours. Meg would become a foster parent, a status she associated with overworked and selfless families from the Bronx and upper Manhattan. She would accept subsistence money for her charge. By strict definition, she would be paid to perform the service of child care. Then she would attempt to adopt. Since her therapy with Libby, since she had articulated her position on parenthood, Meg was eager for the opportunity to provide for this child, to leave Kimble alone to decide who she would be, to guard the gate while she passed in and out of it, eventually through it. Yet the agency that would effect Kimble's adoption, emissary of society's most righteous presumptions about parenthood, would judge Meg as the woman who would possess Kimble. In their eyes, she would be seeking the right to own a human being. They would investigate her qualifications to *own* Kimble. She would be in competition with people whose credentials had the dull sheen of propriety. The investigation would be scrupulous and openly rivalrous. As Meg ran across Canal on her way to Duane, her collar now soaked, she wondered if this investigation might wear down her evolved vision of motherhood, a hard-won vision she had yet to put into practice. If she had to fight so hard to gain custody of Kimble, how would she then resist the urge to possess her?

As Meg mounted the cement steps to her building she saw Jeb, Chris's son—14, maybe now 15—with a girl. They were leaning up against his father's truck that was parked in front of their building. The girl had a nose ring, and Jeb had pushed a length of ribbon through it. He now peeled the ribbon into three strands for braiding. The girl giggled as Jeb braided, but he also tugged between efforts, and each time he tugged the girl yelped and pressed herself harder against the truck door. "Stop, Jebby, you're hurting me," she begged. Jeb laughed. "I'm sorry, but this is going to be so cool," he said.

"Do you want the elevator held?" called Meg, purposefully announcing her presence in their midst.

Jeb, guiltless, turned around. He held the braids in place. "That's OK, Meg," he said.

Meg, to her disgrace, felt oddly privileged that Jeb had interrupted his first, misguided seduction to acknowledge her by name. She paused before putting the key in the lock. She had stopped running only a quarter of a block away; her pulse ticked in her throat. "Remember Kimble?" she called to Jeb. "The little girl you baby-sat for? She's coming to live here permanently. I just got legal guardianship."

"Cool," said Jeb. He held on to the braids looped through the nose ring. The girl stared ahead stiffly, said nothing.

"So no bouncing your basketball on the ceiling after her bedtime, OK?"

"Me?" asked Jeb, and then turned to the girl. "She's talking about someone else," he assured her.

∞   ∞   ∞

Upstairs there was nothing Meg could do to distract herself from a whirling, painful anticipation that seemed to alter the essence of the most familiar objects—recomposing their atoms, it seemed, so that they assumed treacherous new characters. Meg knew about the regenerative powers of anticipation. In the past, when expecting a call from someone to whom she was deeply attracted, the most common objects around her—a

crumb-filled toaster oven, a dustpan tucked into a corner—
became talismans; they abandoned their functions in order to
hold Meg's overbrimming expectations. By the next week, or
maybe the next day, they had regained the dull purpose of their
design. Meg was always relieved when they did so.

Today, this afternoon, nearly everything Meg laid her eyes
on was transformed. The ceramic Hera, half wrapped, was
charged with tidings both ecstatic and grim. It reflected the
conviction of her run uptown: that Kimble's arrival would jolt
her into claiming her full life—more focused work, luck in
love—and then her downtown run—deflation, a belief that
nothing really changes. Hera and every other object in Meg's
view swelled with tale bearings, with reckless predictions. Meg
headed for her bath, where she closed her eyes in defense
against these objects. She took a long time soaping and scrub-
bing, her eyes closed all the while. After she got out and quickly dressed, she opened the drawer in the kitchen island,
removed a package of colored balloons, and blew up as many as
she could.

Minutes later, when she opened the downstairs door, she
had not fully regained her breath. There on her doorstep were
Mrs. Cheney and Kimble. Kimble's mouth moved as she said
something. All Meg heard was the girl against the truck: "Jeb,
this isn't funny anymore, let me go!" The ribbon braid now
trailed down to the street, its end slapping the curb as Jeb continued his work. Meg wanted Kimble to repeat herself but
knew better than to ask. Still, she wished she had heard Kimble
the first time. To have one private moment, one uninterrupted
moment that might resemble the shape it had borne in the
imagination, this was impossible on the streets of New York.
She cast Jeb and his girlfriend a look of disgust.

"They're making progress in the fight against adolescence,"

said Mrs. Cheney. "The CDC has finally recognized it. Soon the parents of adolescents will be entitled to benefits."

Was this the same officious woman who had done the home study? Meg wondered if by passing muster with the city she had given Mrs. Cheney the liberty to reveal her personality.

"That's something to look forward to," responded Meg. She saw that Kimble was staring at her. "Where's Roller Queen, honey?"

Immediately Kimble's neck grew mottled. Her face turned red. Mrs. Cheney squeezed her shoulder. "Private ownership is not a concept most of our children recognize," she apologized. "I'm sorry. There were two other children in the home. We're not sure exactly what happened to that doll, but I have my suspicions."

Meg took them upstairs. On the way, pointing out to Kimble the pictures in the elevator that were new, she tried to reconcile herself to the loss of Roller Queen. She did not utter her name but wondered how Kimble could possibly sustain this new loss, how she herself could sustain it. She had rarely seen Kimble without Roller Queen, and she had repeatedly observed the intensity of their relationship. Meg had seen Roller Queen naked, her peaked breasts and the undivided mound between her legs buffed to a polish by the satin panties that Kimble pulled on and off her at whim. She had seen her face streaked with slashes of Magic Marker—Kimble's anger that could not be entrusted to anyone else. She had seen Roller Queen return from Grandma Shirl's looking like anybody's little slut and had helped Kimble to wash the foundation and rouge and lipstick from her face, all the while telling Kimble that athletes like Roller Queen usually preferred a natural, wholesome look. Once, when she had gone back to the futon to check on Kimble's sleep, she had seen Roller Queen at the foot of the bed, a cut-out Princess Di suit and wide-brimmed hat neatly taped to her plastic form. The Dover Book of the Royal Family had been thrown across the floor, as had Kimble's clothes, but Roller Queen looked crisp and tidy, fully prepared to accept the adoration of the world. It had been Roller Queen and Roller Queen alone, whom Kimble had spared from her rampage with the black tempera paint. Even Meg, while hardly giving her a conscious consideration, had grown to think of Roller Queen as a charmed presence—like Hera, a protectress of considerable influence. The difference was that Roller Queen was new to the world, and as charged as Kimble's love had been, it was not the ancient love of myth; Roller Queen was an object that had vanished, at least for Kimble, and they could not turn her into myth using merely their private sorrow.

When Meg opened the door to the loft, five balloons bobbed along the floor at their feet. Kimble watched them but said nothing.

"They're for you," said Meg. "To welcome you home." She felt the incredible paltriness of the gesture. "This will be your real home now."

"The balloons will be my real home?"

"Silly. This loft, my loft, will be your real home. Our loft, now."

"The lady at the foster home had balloons. For my birthday."

Frantically, Meg turned to Mrs. Cheney.

"Sing your new song for Meg," said Mrs. Cheney.

Kimble looked put-upon but nonetheless opened her mouth to sing, more to recite, "One is none, two is you, three's not me, four's a bore, but five is alive, and I am five." She did a small and dilatory dance, exuberant steps gone flat from too much performance.

Mrs. Cheney nodded. She looked at Meg and whispered, "Mrs. Marzola told us."

"My God," mouthed back Meg. How was it she did not know Kimble's birthday? This child she was trying to adopt—how could this be?

"Five already!" Meg now declared. She might have been a hale and hearty stranger on a bus.

"The lady wanted to buy me a new Roller Queen, but she said she couldn't. But she gave me glow-in-the-dark stars. And I got a chocolate birthday cake, but no Ho Ho's. I know who took Roller Queen, anyway. It was Angel Rivera. He's got this ugly long fingernail, and he screamed when the lady tried to cut it. He took Roller Queen and cut up her eyeballs with his fingernail and threw her down the 'cinerator, so she went headfirst down a really long chute and then burned to death in a burning fire."

"How unpleasant for her," said Mrs. Cheney.

Kimble did not talk like this before is what Meg wanted to say. Charlotte, though, would have said precisely that and would not have restrained herself from adding that terrible things went on in foster homes. It was true that Meg had not heard Kimble talk like this before, but she had heard Juliet Tree's children—little angels cradled by water wings in the deep end of the pool at the White Plains Swim Club—she had heard them talk exactly like this.

"Would you like to see the kids from the REACH playroom?" asked Meg. "Jackie and Tito and Paulie and Kevin? Chantelle?"

"Yes. Are they here?" Kimble craned her neck to see around the corner.

"No, but I could invite them to celebrate your birthday. You could have two birthday parties; there's nothing wrong with that."

Just as Kimble nodded, Meg realized she might have to renege on this impulsive offer. Ray had kept her up-to-date on all the kids: Kevin's mother had died, and he had moved to Georgia with his Aunt Gwyn. Paulie was in the Foundling Hospital; his foster mother had told Meg he was too much for her—this new incontinence and the constant draining of the Hickman. And since the home-care workers started coming, things were missing—her mother's cameo from the Ponte Vecchio, just gone. Jackie and Tito were doing pretty well, but Chantelle had gotten PCP again. Then two weeks after her recovery, she had shown up at the REACH playroom with weeping sores on both cheeks. She had sat in a cherry-colored plastic chair, speechless and perfectly immobile, Ray had said, and the bright sores had been the same color as the chair.

"And Ray Sting Ray? He'll come too?"

"If he possibly can, I'm sure Ray will be there with bells ringing."

"Miss Krantz," interrupted Mrs. Cheney. "Could you sign some papers before I go?"

Meg had forgotten about Mrs. Cheney. Now she studied her, looking for signs of her unease at releasing Kimble into this provisional world, a place where the faces of children erupted into harsh topographies without warning. Whatever Mrs. Cheney was thinking, whether she was disparaging of Meg's chances for adoption or calculating how quickly she could go home, Meg looked at her and said, "When I was a kid I hated Mary Poppins. All that moralizing and enchantment offended me. But I remember this one scene in which Mary Poppins takes the Banks children to see her friend the sidewalk artist. Bert, I think his name was. He had drawn in colored chalk this pastoral scene on the London pavement. He told them how to enter the scene, and they did. They wandered around—really, sort of wafted around—eating ice cream. I was a cynical child, and I made cynical noises whenever anyone read me this part. But later I always sneaked out of bed and read the scene over to myself and stared at the picture of Mary Poppins and the Banks children in Shangri-la. I closed the book before the part where Mary Poppins leads everyone back to reality. Now I wish I were Mary Poppins."

Mrs. Cheney snorted, maybe at the notion of Meg in a calf-length skirt, an umbrella primly hooked over her arm. "Yes. I know what you mean. A Mary Poppins who simply forgets to lead everyone back to reality."

∞   ∞   ∞

Meg's van was stopped at a light on the corner of Park Avenue South and 17th Street. It had been dark for almost two hours. Kimble wore a new jacket, a ski jacket with a fur-lined hood that someone had donated to the group home. She sat with her arms locked tightly about Hera, who was swaddled in bubble wrap.

"Aren't you warm, sweetie? Don't you want to take your hood down?"

"No."

Meg could barely see Kimble's face. In the hours since Mrs. Cheney's departure, Meg had not had the chance to really look at Kimble. She had been amazed at how canny a five-year-old could be at finding ways to avoid eye contact. First she had jumped on her new bed so that her hair waved from one side of her face to the other. Then she had spent a good 20 minutes scanning her new room for bugs. She did this by pointing her finger like a divining rod into every corner of the room, both on the floor and at the ceiling, chanting, "No bug, no bug, no bug."

Her concentration had been absolute. Next, she became preoccupied with a kaleidoscope Meg had picked up at a sidewalk sale the week before. She walked about the loft with one eye fixed to the kaleidoscope's eyepiece and the other tightly shut. She had groped the walls with one hand. Meg had let her do this but had meanwhile tried to observe her, to see if the group home had changed her. In general, Kimble was not the slight, waxy-skinned little girl who had accompanied Barry Toffler to the Central Park Zoo that day of their first meeting. Barry had been visibly reduced, a man whose muscles had atrophied under the dreary weight of his fatigue. Only the way he spoke, in measured growls from the side of his mouth, had suggested his former toughness. Kimble's wispy appearance had seemed to mimic her father's decline. Meg remembered that at first glance she had been taken aback at the thought that Kimble was wasting too. Now Kimble seemed to be transmuting into another physical type altogether. Her blond hair was thicker. The former suggestion of a widow's peak at the tip of her forehead had grown more pronounced. (Charlotte liked a good widow's peak. A good widow's peak, she had often said, was a sign of shrewd intelligence.) Kimble's very skin seemed thicker; Meg was no longer reminded of the close proximity of her organs.

"How can my mother see how pretty you are if you don't take off your hood?" A grown woman alluding to her mother while talking to a motherless child, thought Meg. Shouldn't there be an ordinance?

"She doesn't have to see me."

"You're going to give her that very important pot. I made it for a friend of hers. She'll want to see your face when you give it to her."

Kimble said nothing. She turned her head away to look out the window. Each time they passed under a green light Meg

noticed that Kimble tipped her head to the side. Counting.
Registering. Confiding. Meg parked the van in a garage. She
asked Kimble to give her Hera, just until they got up to
Charlotte's floor.

The doorman called up to Charlotte's apartment. He
repeated Meg's name into the house phone several times. Meg
waited, regarding the doorman's placid expression. She couldn't
remember his name but knew it was the name of a God. Zeus?
Of course not. Now he was quiet, listening to her mother. He
pulled a loose thread from the buttonhole of his jacket. Apollo?
Hermes? Finally he nodded them up.

It was nearly 8 o'clock, and Meg had not thought about dinner. After she gave Hera to Charlotte, she would suggest they
order in. Kimble tended to become cheerful in the presence of
food in white cartons.

"Well!" Charlotte called from the open door. "This is a
moment, isn't it? A real moment." She looked only at Kimble,
still hooded.

"I'm sorry, I really should have called. They said things were
ready, and before I knew it, there she was at my doorstep."

Charlotte touched Kimble's hood. "This is a bit on the
nasty side, isn't it?" she asked, holding the material between
her fingers. "We have our work cut out for us, it seems."

Her mother was drunk. Not a single word was slurred, but
each was drawn out over a luxury of time she allowed herself.
Each word was an act of discipline, its laborious pronunciation
goading it into the next word. She was wearing a kimono with a
lacy plum-colored bra underneath. Meg knew the bra came
from Victoria's Secret. For the past several years her mother's
lingerie had been a topic of conversation. During their monthly lunches Charlotte had often described her new undergar-
ments. Before she finished her description, her playful tone had

usually mutated into a contentious one. Her sexy underwear was the gift she offered her aged body and the act of defiance she imposed on the world that would not have it.

It scared Meg when her mother drank, but she could not imagine saying so. She looked at her, stared at her bloated face.

"Of course she's an alcoholic!" Libby had burst out when Meg told her about the weekend afternoons. "You believe this only-on-Sundays business? So what—so the old dame's an alcoholic, wallowing about with the other swine. I'm glad she has an interest."

Meg had despised this, had accused Libby of producing drama where there was none.

"So she's an alcoholic," Libby had repeated. "Half the people in this country are alcoholics. Some entrepreneur needs to set up recovery centers in the malls. You know, little kiosks. The alkies could stop in for a quick run through the 12 steps. It's the only way. Meanwhile, what are you going to do about Mom?"

This had been a question to be ignored—merely one of Libby's routine challenges. Now, though, Meg wanted to call to Libby, the Libby inside the pot she held in her arms; she wanted to continue their meandering deliberation, the swirling dialogue that seemed only by chance to strike upon and rephrase the few constant themes of their work together. Watching Charlotte approach the living room so unsteadily, Meg wanted nothing more than to sink deep into Libby's blue recliner. She wanted only to describe what she now observed, describe it with the particular attention to detail that would transport her onto another ground.

"Mother, she likes that jacket. If she likes it, she can wear it. What do we care?" Meg spoke to Charlotte's back.

Charlotte turned, sat clumsily on a side chair, and attempted to cross her legs. "Meg, I'm sorry. This is hard for me. The standards of my generation, my standards for years. How much can I fight myself?"

"I'm not asking you to fight yourself. I'm asking you to relax. Please. So the jacket's a little ugly. It will not snuff out whole populations. Where do you want this?" asked Meg, holding out the pot.

"There is fine," said Charlotte, and pointed to a sideboard.

Meg knew what was behind its curved mahogany doors. She waited.

"Would you like a drink, dear? Kimble could have juice. I have cranberry juice."

This is what Meg wanted to ask Libby: *If I say, "No, I don't want a drink, the fact is you drink too much"—If I say that, what then? Do I have to go down with her to the place where she finds out why she drinks too much? If I am the one who says the words, how can I just leave her with them?* This had always been the question.

Libby would have said: *You most certainly can leave her with just those words. Adults can do that with each other. Trust each other to meet their own occasions.*

"Mother, it's dangerous for you to drink alone. You could fall. You could leave something burning on the stove. You could start a fire."

"Oh, I'm fine in here, these buildings were built to last."

Her legs seemed to uncross of their own accord. They drifted apart.

Kimble leaned to the left, her gaze drawn to the dappled white flesh of Charlotte's inner thighs.

"I know you think I'm a terrible snob. I'm a snob because I can't abide a pink polished cotton hood with a dirty little fake-fur fringe. You don't dare breathe a word today. You have to apologize for having standards."

Meg did not say anything. What would she have to apologize to Kimble for in the years to come? What aspect of her character, so habitually clung to, would she have to suppress, to fight, in order to win her daughter's favor? Would she apologize to Kimble for her stubborn insistence on the uncomfortable claw-foot tub, the adobe-colored refrigerator with the fountain in its door?

"Meg-leg, I'm hungry," complained Kimble. She touched Meg's arm.

"Let's all go out, Mother. Get dressed. Let's all go out and get some air."

"Out?" repeated Charlotte.

"Yes. The idea is we'll go out and you'll get some air. Dress warmly."

As soon as Charlotte reappeared in her mink coat and her Joan David calfskin boots, her hair absurdly moussed, the three of them left. Meg locked her arm within the crook of Charlotte's, like a brace, and they walked along. She held onto Kimble's hand too. They turned on Lexington Avenue and walked in silence, adjusting to the bite of the wind, the sound of the traffic. Finally, struggling to maintain the most neutral tone, Meg asked, "Do your friends drink?"

"Oh, my friends," said Charlotte. Then, after a moment, "Grace Spitzer had a colostomy. The poor thing has one of those bags."

"McDonald's!" shouted Kimble, shaking off Meg's hand.

"This is her first day back," Meg said to Charlotte. "I guess we have to do it."

"McDonald's?" asked Charlotte.

"I'm sorry, yes."

"I could have made a reservation at Trader Vic's," said Charlotte. "Or even Café des Artistes. They have that wonderful

dessert plate children love. This is a night to celebrate!"
Charlotte's tone had regained some strength, but now it
momentarily caught.

"Those aren't the kinds of desserts she likes," said Meg,
thinking of the pasty almond tart, the dense wedge of German
chocolate cake.

They entered McDonald's. Immediately Meg realized she
had never been in a place of such lurid color with Charlotte.
Certainly they had never stood together in a room lit so harsh-
ly, lighting that struck their unaccustomed eyes like a blow.
They had never walked together into a place filled with bright
Formica tables or a place where cheerful plastic letters spelled
out copyrighted food names from a backlit marquee.

Once at their places, Meg unwrapped her scarf and took off
her own and Kimble's jackets. Raptly focused on the food tray
before her, Kimble was cooperative: Her arms became pliant as
clay. The day of the Sullivan County Crafts Fair came back to
Meg: the rest-stop bathroom stall; the bluebird-patterned
underpants; Kimble's exposed, formless legs and how she lifted
each one in trustful subordination as she stepped into stiff new
jeans, clothes as unfamiliar to her as if they were the costume
of another land. Now, here at McDonald's, Kimble put her
hand on the top of her pink hood protectively, then let it fall
away as Meg removed the jacket. She set right to eating.

Charlotte sat also, but kept on her mink coat and did not
unwrap her Filet o' Fish sandwich. She drank some coffee and
watched the people around her: a man in a stocking cap who
tore apart some sugar packets, the pregnant teenage girl beside
him. Meg sat also and began to speak about Hera—how she
had used the techniques of the Nigerian Ibibio potters to dec-
orate her; how, if she were going to be audacious enough to create fertility images, the least she could do was pay homage to

people from cultures who had historically prized these images. By contrast, Meg explained, her American customers (Juliet Tree included) attended New Age retreats in the Catskills and fell into a sudden and ferocious swoon of goddess worship, a fervor Meg knew to be spawned by their recalcitrant ovaries.

Then, as if she herself were drunk and without inhibitions, Meg confessed, "I feel like such a hypocrite, taking money from these women I don't respect. I feel so guilty."

"My God," said Charlotte. "What have you done wrong?" She looked up, her eyes less bleary. "Tell me what crime have you committed—giving people something to believe in for a moment? These women aren't so stupid as you think when you're being cynical, Meg. They buy your fertility goddesses because they can't stand that they have nothing to believe in. They're worn to a nub by their own drive to possess, take my word for it. They like to be reminded that someone, some-where, believes. Who knows what your pots might spark in them, might be the beginning of? Do you really suppose that they think your jugs and pots will bring them babies?"

Kimble, looking a little frightened, tried to stick a french fry up her nose.

"Don't do that, honey," said Meg. She had an impulse to argue with her mother, to show herself up as truly mercenary, but she saw that Charlotte was fully prepared to disarm the pose that most held Meg down: her readiness to condemn her-self. In her fading drunkenness, Charlotte had sat across from Meg, as Libby had done, and described what she saw.

"If you're done with those, then put them aside," Meg told Kimble, who fingered the end of the french fry coming out of her nose. Meg took hold of her wrist, and the french fry dropped to the ground. Kimble looked panicked, then began to wail. This child who had passed obligingly from mother to father to stranger to city welfare system now wailed at the loss of one french fry from a bag whose contents she had already accounted for. Meg instantly saw the loss as Kimble did, and she turned to her mother.

"She's exhausted," said Charlotte, bending to pick up the french fry. When she straightened, her mink coat fell open, and Meg saw that although her mother had put on a linen blouse, she had neglected to button it. All there was for Meg and Kimble to look at was the lacy plum-colored bra from Victoria's Secret.

People were entering McDonald's from behind them. It occurred to Meg that if she waited but a second, the cold rush of air that trailed behind these people would hit Charlotte's bare chest and inform her of her predicament.

"Mother," she said, before the people and their air could reach them. She gazed ahead.

"Oh, dear. Look at me," said Charlotte. She closed her mink.

Kimble's crying barely subsided before she began to laugh. Her laughter turned to gleeful hysteria.

"This would not have advanced your standing at Trader Vic's," said Meg.

"Would you excuse me while I go to the ladies' room?" asked Charlotte. With excruciating self-possession, she stood and walked toward a door near the glaring marquee.

"Come here," said Meg to Kimble, who sat with her cheek on the table, heaving, trying to recover from a wave of laughter that had left her hiccuping.

The lights and colors of McDonald's vanished when Meg closed her eyes. She patted her knees. Without protest Kimble climbed onto Meg's lap and sat there until she regained her wind, enough to set off another gale of hysteria, laughter whose vibrations rumbled against Meg's ribs and into her spine. The resulting sensation was amplified, extravagant, piercing—what a mother must feel when the baby on her breast for the first time opens its mouth to laugh.